WITHDRAWN
DATE

EARTH'S VANISHING FORESTS

Also by Roy A. Gallant

Roy A. Gallant

EARTH'S VANISHING FORESTS

Macmillan Publishing Company
New York

Maxwell Macmillan Canada
Toronto

Maxell Macmillan International
New York   Oxford   Singapore   Sydney

For Deb and Jim

Macmillan Publishing Company is part of the
Maxwell Communication Group of Companies.
Macmillan Publishing Company
866 Third Avenue
New York, NY 10022
Maxwell Macmillan Canada, Inc.
1200 Eglinton Avenue East
Suite 200
Don Mills, Ontario M3C 3N1
First edition
Printed in the United States of America

10 9 8 7 6 5 4 3 2 1

The text of this book is set in 11 point Baskerville.
Book design by Constance Ftera

Library of Congress Cataloging-in-Publication Data
Gallant, Roy A.
   Earth's vanishing forests / by Roy A. Gallant.
      p.   cm.
   Summary: Discusses the ecology of rain forests, the problem posed
by the present danger to rain forests, and possibilities for the
future.
   ISBN 0-02-735774-0
   1. Rain forest ecology—Juvenile literature.   2. Deforestation—
Environmental aspects—Juvenile literature.   3. Man—Influence on
nature—Juvenile literature.   4. Rain forest conservation—Juvenile
literature.   [1. Rain forest ecology.   2. Rain forest conservation.
3. Man—Influence on nature.   4. Ecology.]   I. Title.
QH541.5.R27G35   1991   333.75—dc20   91-2624

Tropical forests are disappearing. Somewhere along the road to complete deforestation, people begin to place a high value on the remaining forest.

In most temperate countries, the area of forest cover has already declined to a point at which populations see clearly the value of the remaining forest, and are prepared to protect it. This time will come in the tropics, but if present trends are not reversed, it will inevitably come too late in many cases. Such is the vulnerability of tropical soils to leaching, compaction and erosion under the play of tropical heat and rainfall, and such is the cumulative effect of population growth and economic change, that the forest destruction will be ecologically irreversible and, in many cases, complete.

Many people involved in different aspects of tropical conversion are now acutely worried about the consequences of deforestation.

Others see forests as a more or less inexhaustible source of raw materials, yet their importance goes far beyond the mere appropriation and use of timber, fruits, chemicals or animals.

The forest system fulfills extremely important protective, regulatory and productive functions both for the natural environment and for the well-being and development of society.

The Vanishing Forest:
The Human Consequences of Deforestation
A Report for the Independent Commission
on International Humanitarian Issues

Acknowledgments

I thank Dr. Edward J. Kormondy—friend, ecologist, and chancellor of the University of Hawaii at Hilo—for reading the manuscript of this book for technical accuracy.

I also thank Prime Minister Mary Eugenia Charles of Dominica for extending her hospitality and for expressing her hopes for her beautiful island-nation with its lush and unspoiled tropical rain forest, as unspoiled as its people. My thanks also to Dr. L. J. Charles, Sr., a splendid companion who arranged for introductions, drivers, and guides for various hikes and motor trips through Dominica; television producer Anne Stanaway, who provided companionship and valuable help in documenting the trip to Dominica; and Republic of China Ambassador George Chan and his charming wife, Loretta, who were so hospitable. Phillip Nassief is an enlightened businessman and visionary whose important work is helping Dominica toward the proper kind of development, as is the work of Marshall (Barney) Barnard and his wife Loye, whose love for Dominica has made them a permanent and positive force in the island's culture and economy.

I express my appreciation to the following Dominicans who explained their government's goals in the areas of economic development, forestry, and agriculture: W. Ken Alleyne, General Manager of Dominica's National Development Corporation; Norma Rolle, Promotion Officer in the Division of Tourism; Felix Gregoire of the forestry department, and Phillip Alexander, Manager of Dominica's Tropical Research Center. My list of acknowledgments would not be complete without special thanks to Robert Booth, of the senior editorial staff of *National Geographic*, for his valuable suggestions about where to stay, what to see, and whom to interview on Dominica.

For my trip through the Olympic National Forest and the Cascade Range in the state of Washington, my thanks to my son Jim and his wife, Deb, excellent camping companions. For the excellent photographs credited to the Food and Agriculture Organization of the United Nations office in Rome, Italy, my warm thanks to Giuditta Dolci-Favi, Supervisor of the Photo Library of the Information Division. And finally, my thanks to Four Winds Press (an imprint of Macmillan Publishing Company) for permission to adapt for this book brief excerpts from my book, *Earth's Changing Climate*, copyright © 1979, by Roy A. Gallant.

Author's Note

During an all-day hike through the mountainous tropical forest of Dominica, my guide, John Stoddard, and I paused at the base of a thunderous waterfall whose wild mists dampened and cooled the surrounding luxuriant plants and trees. We just stood there and looked; vour eyes inhaled the spectacle but did not meet—yet each could read what the other thought. After a long silence, I asked him how he would feel if the forests of Dominica were destroyed. He looked at me unsmilingly and said simply, "I think I would die."

Contents

Standing in a crater of an active volcano on the Japanese island of Oshima, I could feel the heat of molten rock beneath through the thick soles of my mountain boots. The rocky earth in all directions was black and lifeless. Steam issuing from a thousand tiny vents added to the eeriness of that desolate and dreadful, lifeless place.

Introduction

SECRETS
OF A
TROPICAL
RAIN FOREST

Many years ago I trudged through the black volcanic desert sands of the Japanese island of Oshima, located an overnight boat ride out into Tokyo Bay. As I stood in the crater of the island's active volcano, Mihara, the plumes of steam issuing from vents in the rock floor were the only sign of activity, a hint of "life" deep beneath my feet. Everything else across the seemingly endless sea of black rock and sand was dead and still. The feeling of desolation and solitude was overwhelming, and I wanted only to leave that alien place.

Dominica's Tropical Rain Forest

As I write this, I have just returned from the opposite end of the world, from the rain forest of that rare jewel of a tropical island, Dominica, not to be confused with the Dominican Republic, a larger island farther north. Caressed by the gentle northeast trade winds, the 29-mile-long and 16-mile-wide island is the peak of an undersea volcanic ridge that is called the West Indies. Most of the island is rain

1

forest, and it has not been spoiled by heavy industry, logging, or tourists. The island is a rarity amid the widespread destruction of most of the world's remaining tropical rain forests.

When I first entered Dominica's rain forest, on what was to be a vigorous six-hour trek to a remote waterfall, I was struck by the difference between the desolate dead world of Mihara and the lush profusion of life in a tropical forest. The hike to Middleham Falls began at the forest edge, where there was an abundance of tall grasses. My amiable guide, John Stoddard, pointed out a medicinal variety, called lemon grass, that grows in thick clusters three or more feet high. I saw banana plants, some harboring young boa constrictors awaiting an inattentive bird in search of insects. There were giant ferns and coconut palms. Towering above the other trees to a height of some 200 feet, with thick trunks five or more feet across, were the giant gommier hardwood trees prized by the Indians as wood for dugout canoes.

Entering the forest from the hot, dry air of the open savannah, I was struck by a wall of cool, humid air that lay heavily on the land. Vines and lianas crisscrossed the forest everywhere, forming a spiderweb network of growth. There were broad-leafed plants with tough waxy surfaces, and there were large, bright red, canoe-shaped flowers about six inches long. The flowers, called balizi, were spotlighted by narrow shafts of sunlight that filtered down through the thick upper story of leaves. Other flashes of color came from the zigzag flight of monarchs and other butterflies.

Unfamiliar sounds caught me off guard, like the creaking and gentle clicking of bamboo trees brushing and knocking against each other as they were stirred by the wind. There were sudden but brief downpours of bulletlike raindrops that crashed and clattered on the forest roof, or canopy. And always, the heavy, damp odor of the forest reminded me of the rapid and continuous decay of the organic matter that paves the forest floor. In early morning, mists hung motionless among the treetops and diffused the light, but by noon the sun was high and cast deep shadows that contrasted sharply with flashing patches of foliage.

The lush growth of Dominica's tropical rain forest is overwhelming compared with the stark emptiness of Mihara. The author takes a breather during a trek to a remote waterfall on a mountain in the middle of the island.

Although I had the feeling that life was everywhere around me, I managed to see only an occasional flying termite or other insect. Bird calls were frequent amid the wind-rustled leaves, but I rarely saw the birds (especially the elusive mountain whistler, which is heard by many but seen by few). Had it not been for an unexplainable feeling of joy and tranquility that the forest provided, I would have been disappointed at not seeing a profusion of animal life. The forest seemed to have a timeless indifference that said: "Here I am to be explored and enjoyed by anyone who cares to know me." The forest just stands there, waiting.

The English naturalist Henry Bates, who traveled through the

Amazonian rain forest in 1848, recorded a similar experience: "We were disappointed . . . in not meeting with any of the larger animals in the forest. There was no tumultuous movement, or sound of life. We did not see or hear monkeys, and no tapir or jaguar crossed our path. Birds, also, appeared to be exceedingly scarce." Like Bates, I was to learn that the forest does harbor mammals and reptiles but that they are widely scattered and secretive; in their shyness they keep their distance from the tread of human feet.

Why Are Rain Forests Important?

Tropical rain forests are the most fragile and spectacular of any forest type. They contain a greater diversity of life than any other place on the planet. An estimated 50 percent of all plant and animal species live in tropical rain forests, although those forests cover less than 2 percent of the globe. Little Panama's forests alone contain as many plant species as all of Europe.

Despite the abundance of life they support, and hence their importance as a natural resource, the forests are being destroyed at a dizzying rate. Most tropical rain forest destruction is caused by land-hungry farmers who first clear the land and then burn what they have cut down. The process is called "slash-and-burn" agriculture and is responsible for the ruin of fifty acres of rain forest every hour. Additional forest destruction is caused by cattle ranchers who clear vast expanses of forest for temporary pasture land. After only a few years the farm plots and pasture land are abandoned because the soil is too poor. Then more forest is destroyed, and the cleared land is used for a few more years before it too is abandoned. When a forest is cut down, its moderating influence is eliminated, which may cause crop devastation in nearby non-forest areas by changing the local climate. This effect is especially probable on large continental land masses such as Africa and South America.

Tropical rain forests are also being destroyed by loggers and by those who ravage the forests for gold, oil, and tin. An estimated one-half million prospectors have slashed their way into the western and northern Brazilian forests and are currently removing some 70 tons of gold a year. As a result, the Madeira River in the north has become dangerously polluted with the mercury used to separate gold from the river-bottom sand. Farmers, ranchers, and miners alike often illegally encroach onto the ancestral land of South American and African tribes whose ancestors have lived on the land for thousands of years. Some of the tribes, whose numbers are decreasing due to murders and disease introduced by the intruders, are on the verge of extinction.

Many people the world over are concerned about the rapid rate of destruction of the planet's tropical rain forests—the forests provide abundant benefits, and they are among the few remaining natural preserves that have not been tarnished by human hands. Not only are they habitats for many animal and rare plant species, but they are important regulators of climate and the source of numerous drugs used to fight disease. Scientists are concerned because so little is known about how a tropical forest works, what makes the forests so fragile, and just how important they are in our lives. Tropical rain forest ecology is a relatively new area of scientific study.

Several institutions are now doing research to find out just how big a tropical rain forest has to be in order to maintain its rich diversity, which is the source of all the benefits it provides. The World Wildlife Fund and the Brazilian government, for example, are conducting a study to find out how well diversity is maintained in forest reserves that range from two and a half acres to 2,500 acres. It will take up to twenty years to measure the effects on the larger forest tracts that have been cut off from their parent forest. So far, the experiment has confirmed what was learned over centuries by trial and error: Smaller reserves do not regain their former diversity once they have been disturbed. Some tropical forest ecologists suspect that a tropical rain forest of less than 125,000 acres, possibly less than half a million acres, cannot remain stable.

Many scientists and nonscientists alike look on the world's tropical rain forests, along with other forests, as vital providers and protectors of the planet. In 1989 a United Nations poll showed that "more than 75 percent of those surveyed in Latin America, Asia, and Africa voiced concern about the loss of trees and woodlands in their homeland and around the world."

This book explores the reasons why people are concerned. Sometimes the reasons are obvious. For example, tropical rain forests are the only source of many medicinal plants that provide us with life-saving drugs; and they are known to be major regulators of local climate. When you disturb the forest, you alter local climate. More often the reasons are less obvious, or even unknown. For example, to what extent do tropical rain forests regulate global climate? And what will be the consequences of losing the major share of plant and animal diversity as the tropical rain forests are destroyed?

1

THE VANISHING
FORESTS

Of all living matter on Earth's land, 95 percent consists of trees and other green plants. The bulk of that vegetation is stored in the world's vanishing tropical forests. Under the hand of man, the forests shrink each year at the rate of about 40 million to 50 million acres, an area nearly as big as the state of Washington.

Why Are the Forests Vanishing?

The agents of destruction are agricultural practices, logging, cattle ranching, mining, the desperate need for firewood in Third World countries, and development. According to a National Geographic Society report, "half of Earth's rain forests have already been demolished, and experts predict that most of what is left will be gone in fifty years or less. With them will vanish a quarter of all life forms—including, perhaps, a plant that could provide a cure for cancer or help end world hunger." The world's ravenous appetite for wood is not new, although the pace at which the growing world population feeds its hunger for wood is new. Since 1960 the world demand for wood has skyrocketed 90 percent, and it is increasing daily.

People have been hacking away at the equatorial rain forests for centuries. The clearing of forests began in order to carry out some kind of agriculture. Africa's tropical rain forests first felt the ax of modern humans at least 3,000 years ago. In South and Central America, prehistoric farmers were clearing their forests some 7,000 years ago. The date is still earlier—some 9,000 years ago—for India and Papua New Guinea, and for Taiwan it is at least 10,000 years ago. In Sumatra planned forest destruction may have started 18,000 years ago, a time when large parts of North America were buried under ice more than a mile deep. Australia's aborigines may have burned sections of a Queensland forest 38,000 years ago. About 70 percent of Europe's woodlands were destroyed before 1850.

The "timeless" tropical forests are not as timeless as many suppose them to be. During the last glacial period, which ended about 10,000 years ago, tropical areas were cooler and drier than they are today. Over a period of several thousand years most of the tropical rain forests of Africa and South America dried up and became open grasslands; only pockets of wet forests remained. Climate change at that time altered the land as much as forest clearing does today. Fertility of the land decreased, soil structure deteriorated, and erosion was common. Then, 10,000 years ago, the great ice melted, temperatures warmed, and rains once again were plentiful. The tropical forests returned. The planet has lost and regained its forests over and over again through geologic time, and the drama will continue, each time with new players and new scenery. Many of the forests we value today are no more than a few tree-generations old.

Needs for Wood

Wood has been, and continues to be, a major fuel source in many parts of the world. In six countries of Africa, wood represents 85 percent of the total energy used. The average figure for the Asian

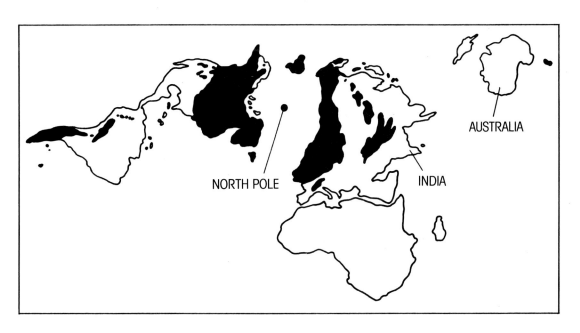

AUSTRALIA

NORTH POLE

INDIA

Top: About 18,000 years ago, at the peak of the last glacial period, ice (dark regions in the diagram) covered about 30 percent of Earth's land surface. Bottom: The Ruth glacier is an example of a mountain glacier and a reminder of what it was like during the last glacial period. This glacier can be seen today in Mount McKinley National Park, Alaska.

nations of China, India, Indonesia, and Nepal is 52 percent; for Brazil, Costa Rica, Nicaragua, and Paraguay, 42 percent. According to the United Nations Food and Agricultural Organization, the number of people in tropical Africa, tropical Asia, and tropical America who no longer have wood for fuel or are using firewood faster than it can be replaced will double to 2.4 billion people by the year 2000.

As demand for fuel wood continues to grow in tropical Third

A farmer carries fuel wood on her back in the Arsi region of Ethiopia. A reliance on wood for energy contributes to deforestation and erosion in Ethiopia and other African nations. Overgrazing by an ever-increasing cattle population also speeds the devastation by erosion.

World countries, wood supplies in the countryside and around cities continue to disappear. In Bhopal, India, for instance, people foraging for wood have degraded woodlands to scrub. Even "protected" parks and reserves are no longer safe from wood poachers. About 70 percent of the wood that is cut in tropical countries is used in homes, mainly for fuel. "In parts of the Himalayas and the African Sahel, [firewood is in such short supply that] women and children spend 100 to 300 days a year gathering fuel wood" (Worldwatch report, Reforesting the Earth). Perhaps nowhere is the problem more extreme than in Africa's Sahel, where women usually walk five to ten miles each day to collect wood to fuel their kitchens.

Deforestation, overgrazing, and long periods of drought have caused the desert to creep over an area the size of Texas and Oklahoma in the Sahel during the past 50 years. In the city of Nouakchott in Mauritania, which borders the Sahara, people sweep their front steps and the streets to stem the daily tide of advancing desert sand. Each year, desertification caused by mismanagement of the land and drought swallows up entire villages and towns in other nations of the Sahel—including Mali, Niger, Tunisia, and Chad. But like forests, deserts have come and gone many times throughout geologic history. According to geologist Farouk El-Baz of Boston University, the Sahara's borders were 300 miles farther south 20,000 years ago than they are today.

Today forested areas of the Sahel region are either gone or fading fast. Niger's forests have decreased 30 percent since 1970 and may vanish in another 25 years. Across the entire Sahel, overcutting has reduced the region's forested area by more than half since 1950. Although it is illegal to chop down live trees in most Sahel countries, the law often is ignored because people are desperate for firewood. According to Mostafa K. Tolba, head of the United Nations Environment Programme, people of the Sahel are reaping a "harvest of dust." He adds that "if the present rate of desertification [in the Sahel] continues, by the end of this century they may not be able to get firewood closer than 900 miles from some major cities, such as Khartoum in Sudan."

Top: Deserts creeping throughout central Africa threaten the lives of cattle and humans alike. Desertification in Chad, part of the Sahel, is making that land one of the poorest and least developed in the world. The dried hides and bleached bones of animals are a common sight. Bottom: Children search for water in an old well in a Tunisian village. Towns like this one are gradually being overwhelmed by the advancing desert. Drought brought on by overgrazing spells doom yearly to millions of inhabitants of the Sahel.

As the Forests Fall

Nearly half of our planet's rain forests have been cut, and most of the cutting has been done since 1960. As late as 1940, the natural forests of Indonesia and Malaysia remained relatively untouched by logging activities. Even in the Philippines, large-scale logging was rare. Between 1910 and 1930, Peninsular Malaysia's rain forests were reduced by three-quarters to two-thirds as the land was cleared to make way for rubber plantations.

Today, every minute of the day and night, almost 100 acres of rain forest fall to the chain saw or are recklessly destroyed by the bulldozer's blade. Many experts fear that most of the remaining rain forests will be gone by the year 2040. Between 1985 and 1988, deforested hillsides in Thailand caused landslides that destroyed the homes of 40,000 people. Thailand lost 45 percent of its rain forests between 1961 and 1985. The disaster awakened the Thai government—it officially banned all commercial logging in its few remaining forests in 1989. However, Thai loggers turned a hungry eye to the forests of their neighbor, Laos. Laos has tough environmental laws, but when large sums of money are involved, corruption, cheating, and theft occur. Despite laws regulating the export of unprocessed logs, clear-cutting of huge areas continues in the Xaignabouli Province of Laos, a region that is under the control of Laotian military officers. Both Laotian and Thai military commanders allegedly pocket large amounts of cash through the illegal sale of unprocessed logs. If you ask Laotian officials about the problem, they simply shrug and deny that it exists. (Perhaps the blackmarket sale of logs has, to their embarrassment, cut them off from tax revenues, which they would rather not reveal.)

In the Philippines the acreage of a prized family of tall trees—the dipterocarps—has shrunk from forty million in 1960 to one-sixteenth that much in the 1980s. Most of the remaining trees stand in remote hill regions and will probably be gone by the mid-1990s. Logging continues in some parts of the Philippines, but it has been stopped in most

Burned tree stumps and devastation mark what was once productive forest and farmland of the Korat plateau in northeastern Thailand. Erosion caused by clear cutting brings flood and drought on the region and its twenty million inhabitants. Loss of the once abundant forest cover has plunged the area into poverty.

provinces. The Philippines lost 55 percent of its rain forests between 1960 and 1985. As of the mid-1980s, one-third of the Philippines' forests had been cut. Much of the forest destruction has been in critical watershed areas, areas that are vital to the collection and storage of fresh water. Cutting on watershed mountain slopes is especially destructive. It causes erosion as water from heavy rains cascades down the barren slopes instead of collecting in the watershed areas. The flood of downslope water then collects soil which flows into and clogs irrigation canals. The rapid storm runoff also floods inhabited lowland areas, and the watersheds become useless as a source of fresh water during the dry season.

In Africa's Ivory Coast, 75 percent of the forests have been cut or burned since 1960. Virtually all of the wood was wasted, representing a loss of about five billion dollars. In Ghana, 80 percent of the forests have been cut or burned, and a scant 15 percent of the timber was harvested before the land was cleared for agriculture. In Brazil slash-and-burn farmers have caused an estimated loss of 2.5 billion dollars a year. Less than half of Peninsular Malaysia's primary rain forest was left as long ago as 1980. Malaysian environmentalists fear that virtually all of their remaining forest will be gone by the time their children are grown. All of the primary rain forests in India, Bangladesh, Sri Lanka, and Haiti have been cut. According to the World Resources Institute, 29.7 million acres of tropical forest were destroyed in eight countries in 1987.

A combination of logging and slash-and-burn farming has brought disaster to the forests of Indonesia and Sabah. Loggers cut, farmers burned, and there was a drought; fires raged from December 1982 to June 1983. Thirteen thousand square miles of forest went up in smoke. During those few months, four years of potential wood exports were destroyed, not to mention the tens of millions of dollars of non-wood forest products. Uncountable species of plants, insects, and birds that grew and lived only in that section of forest were wiped out forever.

Many people who express concern over the rapid disappearance of the world's tropical rain forests suppose that most of the trees are harvested for use as timber. In fact, the reckless use of tractors and other logging equipment destroys 50 to 75 percent of the trees that are not cut. Such destruction has occurred in Sabah, Indonesia, and the Philippines. A logger carelessly cuts down a marked 120-footer, the only tree he is interested in. It comes crashing through the canopy and undergrowth, taking with it nine other trees. The nine other trees are left to rot. A bulldozer next smashes its way to the felled tree to cut a trail for the skidder that will haul the tree out to the road. Both bulldozer and skidder uproot, mangle, and otherwise destroy dozens more trees and churn the forest floor into a mud heap. The manager of one logging operation in Indonesia said that his men take out only about four trees per acre. In the process the forest canopy is destroyed, and about one-sixth of the trees cut down for timber are so damaged that they are left behind to rot.

In other instances regulations have been enacted to protect the forests, but they are either bypassed deliberately or unenforced for lack of forestry personnel. The world's hunger for wood has enabled hundreds of politicians and government workers in high positions to become rich beyond their dreams—in Thailand, Sarawak, Sabah, the Philippines, and elsewhere. The Philippines' Senator Juan Ponce Enrile acquired huge timber holdings when he worked for President Marcos. Most of the more than 500 timber concession holders in Indonesia are retired government officials or military officers who are in positions to persuade the government to ignore logging operation violations or to cover up investigations into illegal operations. Low-ranking forestry personnel who are aware of the violations are helpless—if they speak out they may lose their jobs. Elsewhere, as in Ghana, 50 percent or more of government forestry positions are not filled because of lack of money.

The ideal, from the logging industry's view, is to achieve "sustained productivity," which means cutting and replanting in cycles so that the forests are continually productive. But the forests are not being managed to achieve that goal. In fact, no one knows whether it is possible to coax a forest into continuous cycles of production.

According to a National Geographic report, a representative of an American company cutting in Indonesia was asked: "Will selective logging let the dipterocarp forest survive?" He shook his head. "The first cycle takes the merchantable timber. For the second, say thirty-five years later, the trees won't be as big, and a higher percentage will be, by today's standards, undesirable species. By the third cycle you've radically changed the ecosystem, the birds, the animals, even if no settlers come in."

Ecosystem destruction is rarely a concern of logging companies. Their approach is typically to clear-cut an area, take out the timber of value, and leave the land in a shambles. Or, they may burn what is left

Another centuries-old giant of the Ivory Coast's tropical forest falls to the chain saw. Massive cutting in the 1960s, 1970s, and 1980s eliminated 75 percent of the Ivory Coast forests.

and plant fast-growing trees for use as pulp. More than one such tropical forest "management" scheme has failed because the managers did not apply a simple rule of nature. The big trees that are so prized do not grow close together in groves—they grow far apart from each other. That's why loggers might get only four desirable trees from one acre of forest. Then they learn from painful experience why that is so. They replant a cleared and burned area with a single species of tree, arranging the trees neatly in rows close together. The next thing they know, an insect pest or plant disease attacks one tree and then easily and quickly spreads to the others nearby. In a natural forest, adequate spacing among trees of the same species is a protection against such a calamity. (For a fascinating example of how to *mis-manage* a tropical rain forest, see "Fordlandia: A Foreigner's Dream," page 138.)

Massive Cutting for Massive Profits

Practically all of the mahogany, teak, and other prized hardwood logs in the world come from tropical rain forests. The rain forests also supply about 20 percent of all industrial wood—wood for plywood, pulp, house construction, paper, cardboard boxes, throwaway chopsticks, and disposable baby diapers, for example. The demand for fine hardwood is sixteen times greater today than it was in 1950. The demand for industrial wood also has skyrocketed since 1960.

From the loggers' point of view, tropical rain forests, like any other forest, are to be exploited with little or no concern for environmental consequences. And the best way to exploit them is to cut and sell the trees as quickly as possible. Before a tree can be cut up into a million toothpicks or converted into junk mail, it has to be processed. Most Third World regions—Malaysia and Indonesia, for example—do not have the equipment to convert the bulk of their logs into finished wood products. So they sell the whole logs to Japan, Korea, Singapore, Taiwan, and other countries that do have the equipment and technical know-how. Those countries then turn around and sell the finished wood products at a huge profit. Often the finished wood products are sold back to the country that supplied the whole logs. That practice has gradually been changing in some areas, however. For example, in the early 1960s, Latin American countries exported half their wood as logs. Now practically all of their wood for export is processed.

JANT, a Japanese logging company owned by Japan's Honshu Paper Company, is an example of how big-business over the past 20 years has been devastating tropical rain forests and robbing the countries whose forests they are cutting. In 1973, JANT began clear-cutting 200,000 acres of Papua New Guinea's rain forests. JANT agreed to pay income taxes and royalty money to Papua New Guinea, depending on the profits JANT made by selling the logs it cut. During the 1970s and into the 1980s, JANT cut and shipped to Japan 20,000 tons of wood a month. The company had agreed to reforest the clear-cut areas, but its logging activity has been 10 times faster than its replanting. Furthermore, JANT sold its logs to its parent company back home at such low prices that the company could claim that it did not show a profit. Therefore, it did not pay Papua New Guinea any income taxes or royalty money. Called "transfer pricing," this deceitful business practice has been costing Papua New Guinea an estimated $11 million a year. JANT, by the way, had an agreement with Papua New Guinea to clear-cut an additional 165,000 acres of tropical rain forest after it had flattened the first 200,000 acres.

The countries that sign logging agreements lack the staff to police the logging activity over their huge parcels of forest. This leads to log smuggling, or outright theft. In 1983, about twenty loads of logs were being illegally cut each day from the Ivory Coast's Tai National Park, supposedly a protected area of forest. The smugglers drove their trucks along a road secretly built by a timber company. Elsewhere, poorly defined forest boundaries give loggers an excuse for saying they didn't know they were cutting in protected forest.

Japan had concentrated on importing logs from the Philippines until the Philippines prohibited the export of unprocessed timber. Japan next turned to Indonesia, then to Sabah and Sarawak. In 1990, it began showing interest in moving into the Amazonian forests. According to Robert Repetto of the World Resources Institute, "the Japanese have shown little interest in sustained management of their holdings; they have harvested as much as possible as fast as possible. . . . Moreover, Japanese firms have participated in the bribery, smuggling, and tax evasion that make tropical timber cheap to import and at the same time deprive exporting countries of much of the value of their resource."

As a postscript to this grim tale, author Catherine Caufield tells us that "Japan imports more wood than all other countries combined, nevertheless has two-thirds of its land under forest. . . . Its forests contain enough wood to replace its imports from Southeast Asia and the Pacific for a hundred and fifty years [at 1985 rates of consumption]." Caufield quotes forestry expert Hans Steinlin as saying that Japan's policy is "to protect its forests for as long as possible, although it means over-exploitation of Southeast Asia and the Pacific region."

The future of such Third World nations' forest resources is not hard to predict. Nigeria was once a major exporter of timber, but its supply of wood has virtually been exhausted. Its imports of finished wood products now exceed its exports of logs. Further, it pays more for the finished wood products than it earns from its sale of logs. This crippling economic practice has hurt other developing countries that have mismanaged their precious forest reserves, including Indonesia, Malaysia, the Philippines, and Central America.

Forest Destruction in the Amazon

Brazil's Amazonia contains half of the world's tropical rain forests. The forests grace a region 10 times the size of Texas and provide a spectacle of wilderness beyond the imagination of a city dweller. Only about 10 percent of Brazil's rain forests have been cut to date, but cutting goes on at an uncontrolled pace.

Brazil cites a number of reasons for pushing back its tropical forests. One is political. When boundary lines between nations are poorly defined, and the region where the boundaries are supposed to exist is remote, governments get nervous. If a government does not effectively settle its remote areas, it risks losing them. In 1903 Brazil told its weaker neighbor Bolivia that it was taking over the province of Acre. At various times Chile and Paraguay have also seized parts of Bolivia that were not settled. For the past fifty years Peru and Ecuador have squabbled over 70,000 square miles of border land. Thus governments put roads into such remote land and encourage settlers to clear it, farm it, and squat on it. The settlers need only a dream, a chain saw, and a match.

Some use the word "injustice" to describe the plight of the landless peasants who become settlers. The governments of South America and Central America have long been content to see the rich own and control most of the land, and control the government as well. In Latin America 93 percent of the arable land is owned by only 7 percent of the land-owners. The Volkswagen and Ford companies maintain gigantic Brazilian ranches of low productivity. In Costa Rica, 50 percent of the agricultural land in use is owned by 2,000 ranchers—one-tenth of one percent of the population. In Guatemala, 70 percent of the agricultural land is owned by only a fraction more than 2 percent of the people. Not long ago, 70 percent of Bolivia's farmland was owned by only 8 percent of the people. To this day, the bulk of Bolivia's wealth is held by a small minority of the population. Even though land reform has begun in Mexico, about 5 percent of the farmers there still do not own any land. In El Salvador the figure is more than 20 percent. By contrast, in the Third World country of Dominica, 70 percent of the land is owned by the people. The size of a typical family farm in Dominica is five to ten acres.

Slash-and-burn farming has become the leading cause of tropical rain forest destruction in the world. Every hour fifty acres of rain forest are destroyed by this practice. Most of the burning flares up from the matches of land-poor settlers in Amazonia's Rondônia. In 1987 alone, twenty million acres of Rondônian forests went up in smoke.

Slash and Burn for Hamburgers

The torch was first lit in 1964 by the generals of Brazil's former military government. Then, through the 1970s and 1980s, 15,000 miles of highway were hacked through Brazil's tropical forest and paved in the name of "national integration." The World Bank put up $432 million to help finance the project, called the Polonoroeste Development Project. Then the World Bank stood by and did nothing to correct gross irregularities of forest destruction and the invasion of Indian ancestral lands. The flood of half a million ax- and machete-wielding settlers into the forests during the 1980s made it difficult to prevent unauthorized deforestation and invasion of Indian lands. Since that time, spokesmen for the Worldwatch Institute have said that ". . . the World Bank needs not only to stop funding projects that promote senseless forest destruction, but to more actively support sustainable agriculture and forestry efforts that can relieve pressures on primary forests."

The continued construction of new highways through Brazil's tropical forests channels seemingly endless waves of immigrants who come to fulfill their dreams of land ownership and possible riches from gold or other minerals. They come by foot, mule, bicycle, and cart from the slums of Brazil's overcrowded cities such as São Paulo and from impoverished regions of the northeast. In addition to using Brazil's three major highways—BR-230, BR-429, and BR-364—the settlers have cut countless side roads into the forest in their frenzy to claim free land promised by the government if they "develop" it. "Development" in this case means to clear the forest. The result, say many ecologists, is an "environmental holocaust" and a situation of grave concern to Brazil's new environmentally conscious civilian government that came to power in March 1990. The intrusion of BR-230, the Trans-Amazon Highway, through the forest has been called "a veritable war between man and nature."

Caught up in the frenzy of gaining riches through development, one Brazilian congressman proposed cutting the entire Brazilian forest in the name of "progress." What would the results of such thoughtless action be? According to Jagadish Shukla and Piers J. Sellers of the University of Maryland in College Park, and Carlos Nobre, of the Brazilian Space Research Institute in São Jose dos Campos: "The Amazonian rain forest, once destroyed, probably would not regrow. Cutting the entire forest would severely alter the climate in the Amazon Basin, causing temperatures to rise and precipitation levels to fall—a shift that would severely hinder development of a new rain forest. . . . A complete and rapid destruction of the Amazon tropical forest could be irreversible."

Like the World Bank, the United States has helplessly watched some of its development assistance plans backfire. In the 1960s, the United States financed road construction into Peru's Huallaga River rain forest region in the eastern Andes. The plan was to provide impoverished peasants access to free land so that they could become independent farmers. The plan worked remarkably well, but not in the way the United States and Peru had hoped. The peasants' chief crop on their new land was not maize, squash, or beans, but coca, the leaves of which are processed into the drug cocaine. International drug syndicates quickly moved in. Now the United States is attempting to wage a war on drugs where it once waged development.

There has been no systematic education program to teach Rondonia's peasant settlers how to coax food crops out of the tropical rain forest's poor soil. As a result, their farming attempts are nearly always a failure, and their dreams turn into nightmares. In many cases, one year's crop is all they manage to coax from the soil. During the second or third year the yield is so poor that they move on and "develop"— that is, slash and burn—more forest and try again. Their chief crops are coffee and coca.

The pressure to slash and burn is greatest in those countries where population growth is highest and, therefore, the demand for land greatest. The forested highlands of the Philippines is one such place, where population growth is even higher than the Philippines' already high national average of 2.6 percent. Deforestation and erosion are occurring at a rapid rate. Since it is a Catholic nation, and the Catholic Church opposes contraceptives, the government does not address population control directly. Africa south of the Sahara is another region of rapid population growth, which means damaging stress on the environment. Population growth in Africa is so rapid (2.9 percent a year, and doubling in 35 years) that Africans may make up more than a quarter of the world population late in the next century and maintain their high numbers for a long time, unless famine or disease check their growth. What impact their numbers may have on the forest and other environmental resources remains to be seen.

There are those who play down the seriousness of world popu-

Slash-and-burn clearing is the single greatest cause of tropical rain forest destruction worldwide. The small farm plot here has been burned and cleared and awaits planting on the island of Dominica. Although the Dominican government discourages and controls widespread slash-and-burn activity, the practice is out of control in countries where land ownership by the poor is low and where land-hungry people are many. In Brazil the loss of money from timber due to the wasteful burning of trees is estimated at 2.5 billion dollars a year.

lation growth by pointing to slowing growth rates in European countries. What they fail to realize is that population growth must be regarded as a global problem. They also fail to understand a simple lesson in population arithmetic. An immediate reduction in the growth rate of the world's population would not mean an immediate reduction in the number of people. It would not mean a reduction for many years. Why? Because of a population growth principle called population momentum—the tendency of a previously growing population to keep on growing long after its people stop having a large number of children. (To undersand how population momentum works, see Explanation 1.)

Large numbers of Brazil's rain forest settlers have watched their dreams of becoming independent farmers crumble. Because clearing a tropical forest is hard work, and because malaria and other parasitic diseases often strike, and because year after year of poor crop production is discouraging, many settlers of the virgin forest give up in despair. They then sell their land to wealthy cattle ranchers who live far away in the cities of São Paulo and Rio de Janeiro. The largest such ranches are in southern Rondônia conveniently near highway BR-364.

In Brazil more than 600 cattle ranches average more than 50,000 acres each. The ranchers acquired the land through government loans and tax benefits. Although the government no longer gives such financial aid to new cattle ranchers in the Amazonian forests, it continues to support the existing ranches.

The outcome of cattle ranching in tropical rain forests is as bleak as that of slash-and-burn farming. The settlers who sell their land to the ranchers often are retained as paid laborers to further clear the land and plant grass for pasture. For a few years the grazing is good enough to support the cattle, although meat output has averaged only 9 percent of what many ranchers had predicted. After five or so more years, toxic weeds take over the pastures. Clearing the weeds is too expensive, so the land is once again abandoned, but this time for good. Almost every ranch that was started in the Amazon before 1978 has been abandoned. That land will not see another tropical rain forest for a million years.

And so forest destruction goes on. The only ones to profit from this cycle of forest clearing are the cattle ranchers, who often make up to a 250 percent return on their investment. The peasant farmer-settler loses, and the Brazilian government, which hatched the original plan, is the real loser. Its generous treatment of wealthy ranchers, who hold some thirty million acres of land, has already cost the government more than $2.5 billion in lost income.

Ranching, as practiced on cleared tropical rain forest land and in most of Central America, is wasteful of the land. Meat production may reach fifty pounds per acre a year. By comparison, northern European farms produce more than 500 pounds of meat per acre a year, plus more than 1,000 gallons of milk. Amazonian rain forest ranches do not produce any milk. In Central America more than 25 percent of the forests have been cleared to produce hamburger meat, practically all of which is sold to fast-food chains in the United States. Everywhere in Central America pasture for producing hamburger spreads at the expense of tropical rain forests and of potential farmland for those who are deprived of owning land. The bulk of the wealth in Central American nations remains in the hands of the rich. The large segment of the population that is poor is brutally poor. Land reform, as the fair distribution of land ownership among a nation's population is called, continues to be a serious political and social problem in many countries, especially in Latin America.

Where Do We Go From Here?

While population growth in developed nations shows signs of slowing, populations continue to grow at an uncontrolled rate in most Third World nations. These nations are the custodians of the world's tropical rain forests, and they look on their forests as the most immediate and most promising source of desperately needed income. Do the rich, developed nations, which long ago destroyed most of their forests, have a right to lecture Third World nations on how to manage theirs?

At a 1988 conference in Toronto, Canada, on "The Changing Atmosphere," an African delegate said that he didn't want the Western World, technologically developed and rich, to preach to him about what he could do with his trees, or about what he might be planning in the way of developing his nation. He added that, indeed, it was the turn of his and other Third World nations to develop and generate their share of wealth and the good life. The environment, he said, would just have to be secondary, as it was when the West grew rich by launching the Industrial Revolution. Another delegate to the conference, Minister Emil Salim of Indonesia, readily agreed that the rapid deforestation of his country was not in its best long-term interest. When asked why Indonesia didn't just stop the massive cutting, he replied, "Those trees bring us $2.5 billion of foreign exchange a year that we absolutely need for our development. So if you could provide us with some alternative source [of income], we would be very interested."

Since biblical times mankind has regarded the degradation of nature as its privilege. The health of the environment has always been second. Unfortunately, this attitude is still with us. But there are signs that it may be changing. Concern about the possible effects of tropical rain forest destruction on global climate change is but one sign. Another is the outcry of rage over the destruction of old-growth trees in the United States' majestic forests of the Pacific Northwest.

2
HUMAN LIFE IN RAIN FORESTS

Our ancient ancestors, tens of millions of years ago, made the forests their homes. During much of that time the world was a warmer place than it is now, and a tropical environment was the rule over much of the land. More recently—some two to three million years ago—there were long-term climate changes from warm to cool and back to warm again. Each period lasted about 100,000 years. Although we know something about what happened during those periods of change in the mid-latitudes, we know relatively little about what happened in the tropics. We do know that during the cool periods large amounts of water were locked up as glacial ice and, as a result, sea level was lower. Consequently, much more of the land in tropical regions was exposed for occupation than is the case today.

Over the past 100,000 or more years, countless groups of modern humans have continued to make the forests their home. But whether these forest peoples were able to depend on the forest alone for a living is a question anthropologists have yet to answer. Some scholars think that certain tropical forest groups traded their forest products for food grown or gathered by other groups that lived at the edge of the forest. Perhaps some groups left the forest now and then and supplemented their diet with shellfish and other foods provided by the sea.

Who Were the First Americans?

Africa and Southeast Asia are the oldest tropical rain forest habitats for humans. The forests of Central America and South America were explored and inhabited later. A site in northeastern Brazil, being excavated by archaeologists directed by Niede Guidon, may have had human occupants 30,000 or more years ago. At that time the northern forests of North America and northern Europe were crushed under glacial ice more than a mile thick.

The first tropical rain forest dwellers of the New World apparently crossed over from central and north-central Asia. Waves of these people migrated eastward over a broad bridge of land that has linked Alaska and Siberia from time to time in geological history (most recently about 12,000 years ago). Some of these Paleo-Indian migrants hunted and fished their way southward along the west coast of what is now the United States. Others passed through an ice-free corridor along the eastern edge of the Rockies. The waves of migration occurred over several generations until those bronze-skinned people with mongoloid features occupied virtually all of North, Central, and South America. They were hunter-gatherers who used tools of stone and bone. They were well adapted to living off the land, as are their descendants who continue to inhabit the forests today.

Adapting to Life in the Forest

A few decades ago the discovery of a "primitive" forest tribe living as hunter-gatherers was a major news event. It was thought that few such forest-dwelling groups out of touch with civilization existed. Today we know that many such groups inhabit the world's tropical forests. There are the Bushmen of Africa, about 200 other tribes of

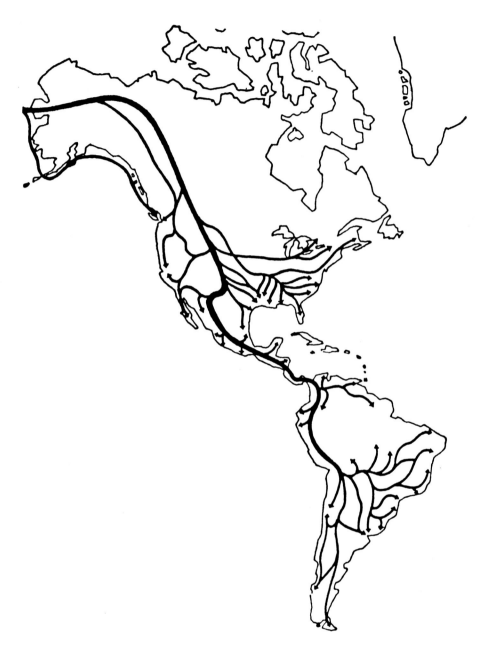

Of the many possible migration routes that the Paleo-Indians and their descendants could have taken to populate North and South America, several suggested by Carl Sauer are shown here.

the Congo Basin, there are the Negritos of Southeast Asia, the Pygmies of equatorial Africa, and some seven million people making up about sixty tribes in the Philippines. There are tribes in Borneo, about 700 tribes in Papua New Guinea, and others in Sumatra, Malaysia, and Thailand. Colombia has sixty tribal groups. According to data collected by Brazil's Goeldi Museum researchers, human diversity in the Amazon forests alone is vast. Of some 170 native languages, anthropologists have fully studied fewer than twenty.

Aboriginal groups who have long made the forest their home have much to teach ecologists. For example, the language of the Kayapos, a Brazilian tribe living in the Xingu Valley, has helped biologists "discover" several new species of bees. Our attitude toward such "primitive" tropical forest tribes has slowly changed over the years from one of pity for the "starving hunters" to one of respect for their adaptation to the forest and their ability to live comfortably and in complete harmony with their natural world. Another misconception about these people has changed—we once supposed that hunter-gatherer groups were isolated from other cultures and entirely self-sufficient. Most such tribes, it now seems, have long had contact with other groups.

The Agta forest people of Luzon in the Philippines, for example, exchange their wild meat and occasional farm labor for rice, corn, and money from their neighbor Palanan farmers. The forest people of Penan in central Borneo seem to have started out as farmers but gave it up and took to the woods about 1,000 years ago when they learned that Chinese traders were hungry for jungle products. Still other hunting groups of Borneo trade resins, beeswax, and medicinal plants for cloth, iron, and transistor radios! The trading, hunter-gatherer groups find it easier to trade for agricultural products than to gather them. Although Southeast Asian rain forests have an abundance of wild yams, bananas, sago, cereals, and other foods, they are widely scattered over the forest and require time and energy to collect. Anthropologists who study the life-styles of prehistoric tribes are finding that such cultural contact among tribes has been going on for thousands of years. Later in the chapter, we will find a detailed example of such interdependence between the Efe, a forest-dwelling tribe, and their Lese neighbors, a farming tribe.

People of the forest have adapted to their environment both physically and mentally. For example, their metabolic rate tends to be slower than that of city dwellers. A slower metabolic rate produces less heat, and so forest dwellers are more comfortable in the hot, humid forest than are people adapted to a colder climate. While hiking in the rain forest of Dominica, I was sweating profusely, but my guide's brow remained dry. I soon discovered that sweating in a rain forest is not an efficient way to cool the body, because the rate of evaporation is so low. Forest people tend to be healthier than most Europeans or North Americans. They have a low rate of heart disease and cancer. Hypertension and stress, common ailments among city dwellers, are rare. Obesity, especially common among both American adults and children, is rare among forest people. Life expectancy among these people, however, tends to be lower than in industrialized societies, because they have little or no medical technology to help them when they are sick. When forest people stop being healthy, they die. Also, because of their relative isolation, they lack immunological defenses against many diseases common among people of industrialized societies.

One lesson forest dwellers learned long ago is that overcrowding usually spells suicide. A given parcel of forest has only so much game, so many fish, and a limited number of food plants. A forest group that supports itself mainly by hunting and food gathering needs one square mile of forest to feed five to seven people. If well-controlled farming is introduced, the carrying capacity of the forest is increased to between 100 and 300 people per square mile. Most forest tribes have learned this ecological lesson and regulate their populations through birth control. Ironically, a number of "civilized" societies have chosen to ignore this law of nature. As a result, they are now experiencing a downhill slide in the quality of life as increasingly large segments of their population sink ever deeper into a state of poverty and poor health.

The Lacandon of Mexico

Farmers of industrialized countries have "conquered" the land with fertilizers, pesticides, and high-yield varieties of food plants. They have highly efficient tools such as tractors and cultivators, and the fossil fuel to power them. Lacking such technology, tropical forest peoples have substituted skill and an intimate knowledge of their poor soils to make a living off the land. For example, a great civilization sprouted out of the Mayan rain forest of Central America. It reached its peak more than a thousand years ago and supported about 14 million people.

Over several centuries the Mayans learned how to manage the soil through trial and error, and through experimentation. Then in the 1500s the Spanish invaders swept down on these people, destroying most of their writings, suppressing their religious practices, and capturing many for use as slaves. During this ruthless conquest and deliberate destruction of a proud culture, many of the Mayans' skills in tropical rain forest management were lost—including their ability to use tropical rain forest land for agriculture without destroying the land or the forest. Because the Lacandon Mayans, descendants of the original Mayans, have adopted many of the ways of their ancestors, scientists have been able to piece together some of the agricultural skills and techniques used by the early Mayans. To this day, the Lacandon Mayans of the Chiapas tropical rain forest of southern Mexico practice farming and use the land with results far better than modern agricultural experts can achieve.

The ancestral Mayans studied the types of vegetation growing on two- to three-acre plots of forest in order to identify desirable garden soil. They recognized some half dozen or more soils of different quality. They looked for certain trees that grew only in rich and well-drained soil. Next they cleared a selected plot and left the cuttings to dry. Several months later they burned the cuttings. The ash, rich in nutrients, was left to seep into and enrich the top layers of the soil. Fast-growing plants such as papaya, chayote, plantain, manioc, and banana were quickly planted to catch the nutrients, prevent erosion, and provide shade for low-growing crops such as sweet potatoes and taro. Next they planted dozens of other crops, including maize (corn), onions, pineapples, peppers, melons, citrus fruit, squash, rice, tobacco, beans, ginger, and avocados.

The Mayans did not stagger the planting time for their various crops on a calendar basis, as modern agricultural practices dictate. Instead, centuries of trial and error taught the Mayans that the flowering time of certain forest plants could be used as a signal to plant tomatoes, rice, tobacco, or one or more of their many other crops. In this way, the Mayans used the forest's natural cycles of rainfall and temperature change rather than a fixed calendar schedule that might not provide the best timing for planting. For example, the farmers knew it was time to plant the spring crop of maize when the mahogany trees lost their flowers. Another key to the success of Mayan farming was the practice of mimicking in their gardens the rich diversity and high density of plants that grew naturally in the forest.

The high density alone would be enough to cause a Kansas corn farmer to choke. There are no neat rows in a Mayan garden. Instead, the dozens of different kinds of food plants are all mixed up, with no two of the same plant type closer together than ten or so feet. Thus disease and insect pests cannot easily spread from one kind of tomato plant to another tomato. Also, the vertical structure of each garden is carefully planned. Root crops such as sweet potatoes hug the ground; higher-growing plants such as maize and sugarcane grow at medium heights; banana plants and papaya trees occupy the upper layers and provide needed shade for the plants below them.

Over hundreds of years, the Mayans and their Lacandon descendants performed countless experiments to find out which combinations of food plants in a garden plot produced the highest yield. They also planted certain crops in order to attract wild and edible animals such as deer, pacas, and peccaries. A Lacandon garden plot supports "spontaneous" forest species (wild pineapple, wild sugar vine) and raw ma-

Colossal stone heads weighing up to 20 tons were carved out of basalt rock by the Olmecs, regarded as Mexico's "mother culture." In 1939 Matthew Stirling of the Smithsonian Institution measured this head, found in Tres Zapotes, at six feet high. Several such heads, of rulers or gods, have been found. The Olmec, ancestors to the Lacandon Maya, occupied Tres Zapotes from 500 to 100 B.C. They were skilled craftsmen, artists, and farmers.

terials used in house construction (balsa and corkwood). The practice of simultaneously producing food crops, trees, and animals on the same garden plot is called agroforestry, and the skills required are not easily taught to newcomers. According to Caufield, "by the time Lacandon children are ten years old, they can distinguish hundreds of edible and otherwise useful plants from those that are harmful."

Destruction of the Lacandon's Forest Home

Until the early 1960s, the spaciousness of their rain forest provided the Lacandon Mayans with treasured privacy, and they lived in tune with their tropical rain forest environment. They gathered wild fruit, hunted the forest's animals, collected natural pesticides to protect themselves and their crops, knew which plants acted as fish poisons, gathered fiber for clothing and ropes, used incense from selected woods during their religious ceremonies, knew which trees made the best furniture and canoes, and readily identified which medicinal plants would ease a toothache or cure a snakebite.

But in 1965 the lives of these people were changed virtually overnight—the bulldozers of timber companies began gouging logging roads through the forest, and rich ranchers began burning vast stretches of forest to make grazing land for their cattle. Today about 450 Lacandon Mayans survive. They live in three villages of perhaps 100 people each; a dozen or more families hide in compounds deep within the forest. Few of the remaining Lacandon have the skills to practice their age-old method of agroforestry. Most find it easier to hire out as laborers and buy their food in stores rather than grow it in their forest home. When the few remaining Lacandon farmers die, their ancient agricultural skills will die with them, for no one else has been taught those skills.

Meanwhile, landless peasants swarm along the logging roads and colonize the Chiapas rain forest. Lacking the skills of the Lacandon, they are rapidly destroying what is left of the rain forest through extensive slash-and-burn farming. Usually, after only a year of raising crops on a few acres of cleared forest, the poor soil can produce no more. The peasants then abandon their plots and slash and burn new ones. Or, they sell their plots to ranchers who further degrade the cleared land in order to raise cattle. The Lacandon farming system can use the same plot for five to seven years. At the end of that time the plot is not abandoned but planted with tree crops including rubber, citrus, and avocado. The plot remains productive for an additional five to fifteen years, during which time natural forest species are growing. When those species dominate, the forest has returned to its former fertility and is ready to be cut and burned again, thus beginning a new cycle. Through this economical use of the forest, a Lacandon farmer may clear no more than 25 acres of virgin tropical forest during his entire life.

Over the past 50 years, more than 150,000 land-hungry peasants in Mexico have slashed and burned their way through huge sections of that country's rapidly disappearing tropical rain forests. The Chiapas rain forest is the largest remaining one in North America. In the early 1960s it covered 5,000 square miles. Today, less than half of it is standing. The Mexican government says that it encourages "development" of the Chiapas rain forest in order to bring the Lacandon Mayans into the mainstream of Mexican economic life.

In Third World countries that have rapid population growth, people pressure is the real culprit. There simply is not enough land to go around. In regions where population growth is not a problem, slash-and-burn agriculture is both efficient and productive. Plots that have been abandoned are allowed to renew their fertility over a period of twenty to twenty-five years; then they can be used again and again. But when the population in a given forest area grows too rapidly, the forest cannot provide enough fresh plots every year. The old plots must be worked almost continuously, with ever decreasing productivity and increased labor.

Worldwide, the growing numbers of slash-and-burn farmers are the single largest cause of tropical forest destruction. There are those who say that we must bring modern technology to the tropical rain forest farmer. James D. Nations, a scientist who has studied the agro-forestry practices of the Lacandons, has an answer to that suggestion: "Rather than eradicating indigenous systems like that of the Lacandon Maya, we should be working with traditional forest farmers as their students. For in the end they will teach us how to farm in the tropical forest without destroying it."

Despite their adaptedness, the way of life and the very lives of many native peoples of tropical rain forests are being threatened as the forests tumble to the tune of the chain saw. Of the 1,300 or so forest tribes around the world, most, if not all, are on the endangered species list. Where they are not being displaced by the logger's saw and the colonist's ax, they are being "corrected" by missionaries and government bureaucrats who want to change their aboriginal way of life, eliminate their languages, and make them abandon their cultures in order to blend in with modern society.

The Wayana of French Guiana

The Wayana Indians, who number fewer than 1,000, live in scattered river villages in north-central South America about 100 miles from the coast. Their home is dense tropical rain forest, and their main highway is the Maroni River, which they travel in long canoes. In the 1700s about 3,000 were driven out of northern Brazil by a warlike group called the Wayapis. Diseases introduced by Europeans, including measles and tuberculosis, had reduced the Wayana's numbers to fewer than 500 by 1950. Since then, improved medical conditions and restrictions on tourist visits have enabled the Wayana to bring their population up to about 800. But other problems—alcoholism and a slipping away of tribal traditions due to increased contact with the outside world—threaten their way of life. Both problems are most evident among the Wayana young people. One source of contact with the outside is a stream of European mining engineers in search of minerals and other valuable natural resources. Wayana males work as guides for the Europeans. The money they earn is spent on outboard motors (for their canoes), guns, radios, kitchenware, jeans, and other "conveniences" that are eroding away the Wayana's traditional way of life.

Wayana houses are perched on posts for protection from crawling insects and rats. The people hunt, fish, and farm. Because the soil is too poor to support permanent fields, they practice slash-and-burn farming, but not with the expertise of the Lacandon Mayans. Their diet of bananas, sugarcane, yams, and other food produced by farming is supplemented by iguana eggs found buried along the river's sandy beaches, juicy insect grubs, large ants eaten live, wild honey, nuts and berries, and smoked lizard meat.

One of the Wayana's food plants, the manioc root, provides a flour (cassava) that is used to make breadlike foods. The root is also the source of their favorite drink, *kasili*. In its untreated state, manioc root is poisonous. The poison can be removed by peeling the root, making a mash, and squeezing out the poisonous juice (hydrocyanic acid). *Kasili* is made by boiling the roots in water in order to remove the poison and form a mash. Women then spit chewed mouthfuls of cassava cakes into the mash. Saliva mixed with the mash speeds the fermentation process. After several days of fermentation, the alcoholic liquid is drained off and consumed by everyone in the tribe, including children.

More than any other aspect of their lives, the Wayana ceremony marking a teenager's passage into adulthood gives the Wayanas their identity. As the ceremony begins, a Wayana youth who has reached puberty is given some *kasili* to dull the pain that is to follow. Meanwhile, many dance as the elders recount tribal myths. Eventually, as many as one hundred stinging ants are spread over the young initiate's body and begin their painful work. The youth is expected to endure the pain by remaining silent and still. Called *marake*, this and other rituals give the Wayanas spiritual strength and provide their strong sense of identity. "The day *marake* goes," said one village elder, "will be the end of the Wayanas."

That day may not be far off. Increasing numbers of tourists flood

into the Wayana villages and, according to anthropologist Carole Devillers, "behave like visitors in a zoo." They pay bare-breasted women
to pose for photographs, and young men to pose with bows and arrows
and other implements that the Wayanas no longer use. Says Devillers,
"The effect on the Wayanas is one of degradation, not merely in their
own eyes but in those of their children, on whom the future of their
culture depends."

The Wayana's counting system goes only to ten and is symbolic of
their outlook on life. Any quantity of objects beyond ten is expressed
simply as "many." "Saving and planning ahead," according to Devillers,
"are strange concepts to the Wayanas—who knows if there will be a
tomorrow?"

The Efe of the Ituri Forest

Pygmy populations inhabit the tropical rain forests of seven African countries. They live in Cameroon in the west and in areas as far
east as Lake Victoria. In all, they number from 150,000 to 200,000
and make up fewer than a dozen populations. Most are members of
hunter-gatherer groups that move from one campsite to another depending on the availability of food. The Efe Pygmies live in Zaire's
Ituri Forest, which contains Africa's richest supply of forest mammals.
This group is another example of a population that is remarkably well
adapted to a hunter-gatherer life in the tropical rain forest. The Efe
average four feet, seven inches in height, and a typical female weighs
about 80 pounds.

The 5,500 or so Efe, noted for their expertise as archers, interest
anthropologists for two reasons. First, their adaptedness to life in the
rain forest is remarkably efficient. Second, the Efe seem to live today
much like the hunter-gatherers of thousands of generations ago. Pygmies are thought to be the first inhabitants of Africa's rain forests.
They probably hunted and gathered food long, long before agriculture
became a way of life. Consequently, the Efe provide a window to our
human past.

As recently as 1989, the Efe had a deep fear of foreigners, thinking that white people eat Pygmies and find their children especially appetizing. When they are encamped, an Efe group may consist of about a dozen huts forming a 50-foot-wide circle, with the doorway of each hut facing the central clearing. A typical hut is built by cutting saplings and pushing the cut ends into the soft ground. A ring of such sapling frames is then bent toward the center and fixed to form a dome. The branches are finely woven to make the dome sturdy. Broad leaves of the mongongo plant are then woven shinglelike into the latticework of branches. When completed, these leafy igloos are watertight and provide each family shelter and privacy. By day, the hut is cool and dark; by night it is warm and lighted by a small fire. Weeks or months later, when it is time to move on because of a scarcity of food, the huts are abandoned and a new camp is set up at a new location.

The Efe hunt either alone or in groups, depending on the game they are after. Their weapons are bows and arrows and spears. Arrow tips may be fashioned of wood and notched to hold a deadly nerve poison, or they may be fashioned of metal. High on the list of their favorite game is the duiker antelope, which they hunt in groups. There are six species of duiker, and a typical kill may weigh about forty pounds. The animal is butchered where it falls, and portions are divided among the hunting party. The largest piece goes to the archer who first struck the animal. Other portions are allotted according to each hunter's contribution to the kill.

An elephant is the ultimate honor for Efe hunters, although elephant hunting is now illegal. (Poachers, however, still kill elephants for their ivory tusks, often employing Efe guides who know how to track the animals.) Before elephant hunting became illegal, word of an elephant kill spread through the forest and attracted neighboring clans for a grand feast. The animal was butchered on the spot and the meat cut into pieces that were immediately smoked to prevent decay. Almost all parts of the animal were eaten, including the prized trunk and the nutritious marrow scooped out of broken bones. Elephant hunting must be a group activity, because it is extremely dangerous;

an elephant kill is a source of great pride for Efe hunters. In all, the Efe hunt more than 45 different animal species to satisfy their diet of red meat.

Along with the duiker, monkeys are common game. About a dozen monkey species are hunted. This is a solitary activity because monkey hunting requires shrewdness and quiet. The lone hunter carefully prepares his poisoned arrow tips and quietly waits for a troop of monkeys to come his way as they forage through the forest canopy. He then begins shooting his arrows, missing most of the time. One hit for eighteen arrows shot seems to be the rule. Of all the forest animals hunted, monkeys provide the most meat per hunting hour.

Wild honey is another favorite Efe food. Honey gathering is a seasonal activity, and the availability of honey varies from one year to the next. In a good year a half dozen or so hunters may spot about 15 hives during an hour and a half of foraging. The hives usually are high above the ground in tree hollows. A hunter, carrying glowing embers that are wrapped in moist leaves and packed in a basket, climbs to the hive entrance, which may be 60 feet or more up in the canopy. The clump of smoking leaves is held by the hive entrance, and as the smoke enters the hive, its bitter odor overcomes the bees long enough for the climber to reach in and break off sections of honey-laden cone, which he then drops into baskets held by his comrades on the ground. Usually the cone sections, dripping with honey, also contain beeswax, larvae, and pollen, all of which are eagerly gulped down. The hunters may gorge themselves until their stomachs bulge with a pound and a half or so of honey, wax, and larvae. According to one researcher, honey provides 14 percent of the total calories brought into camp by the Efe. Another insect delight is roasted termites pounded into a paste—it is eaten as trail food during a move to a new campsite.

It has been said that the Efe know their forest home as well as any city dweller knows his neighborhood. "Blindfold an Efe hunter and walk him for hours into the forest. Remove the blindfold and he will recognize individual trees and other forest landmarks and immediately retrace his footsteps home." The Efe are as at home in the forest as their neighbors living in Lese farming communities are terrified of it.

The Lese live in villages at the forest's edge and are as skilled at farming as the Efe are at hunting. The Lese are in touch with the outside world and now use modern kitchenware and tools such as axes and knives. The two groups have come to depend on one another for their mutual well-being as surely as other organisms that have adopted mutualism as a way of life, although the association of the Efe and the Lese is a social form of mutualism.

Like the Efe, the Lese prize meat, but they are not hunters. The Lese tend to view the Efe forest people as socially and biologically "inferior." The Efe are sensitive to and resent this prejudice; nevertheless, the two groups coexist in harmony. Although a Lese man may take an Efe woman as his wife, Lese women feel superior and will not marry Efe men.

In times of plenty, the Efe give meat to the Lese in exchange for garden foods and pots and pans. When times are hard for the Efe, they work as laborers in the Lese's garden plots. So close is the interdependence between the two groups that many Efe and Lese individuals regard themselves as associates. Anthropologist Robert C. Bailey, who has studied the Efe extensively, quotes one Efe hunter as saying: "Abamu is my *muto*—my villager. We always help each other. I bring him meat and honey and help him clear his garden. He gives me garden food and helps me buy clothes and other things. My father and his father helped each other in the same way."

Despite their adaptedness to the forest, two-thirds of the Efe's calories are grown in Lese gardens. Bailey speculated that the Efe might not survive for long without trading forest resources and labor for garden foods. He further points out that "the forest, as lush as it appears, does not have the density and abundance of edible resources to sustain human foragers for long periods." This probably has always been so—tropical forest dwellers, despite adaptation to their forest environment, may have depended on trade with farming groups ever since agriculture was well-developed more than 10,000 years ago.

As the fate of the Wayanas seems threatened by the intrusion of modern civilization, what may be the fate of the Efe? Despite their adaptedness, life is harsh for them, at least by our standards. Both Lese and Efe children are hard hit by dysentery, malaria, and other diseases caused by parasites. Many infants die before their first birthday. In addition to their health problems, which the Efe have endured for centuries, the Efe face a new threat to their existence—the gradual shrinking of their tropical rain forest home. The Efe are no longer in a position to control their own destiny. The very large areas of forest they require to support themselves are being cut around them. Helplessly, they watch their forest home shrink. Zaire's rapid population growth is one cause. The annual population increase is 3.3 percent (the world average is 1.8 percent). Each year, as ever greater numbers of land-hungry Africans seek free land on which to cultivate crops, the Efe's forest domain is pinched tighter. Their fate is tied to the forest itself. Unless forest land is set aside for them, this unique and ancient culture will be lost forever, along with our opportunity to learn about our beginnings and our cultural evolution as a species.

Brazil's Vanishing Indian Cultures

Nowhere in the world is there such widespread destruction of tropical rain forests as in Brazil's state of Rondônia. By 1990 an estimated 20 percent of Rondônia's forests had been cut by loggers or slashed and burned by a flood of impoverished settlers who were offered free land by the government. Some settlers chase their dreams of finding gold in the mineral-rich state, but most try, unsuccessfully, to farm the infertile soil. Malaria strikes down many. 240,000 cases of malaria were reported in 1987; this figure represents 20 percent of Rondônia's population. After two or three years the settlers usually give up farming, leaving only destruction behind. Damage to the environment has been severe.

During the 1980s Rondônia's population doubled. By 1988 200,000 settlers' children could not go to school because there were no schools. The passion for land ownership runs so high that some

BR-364

BRAZIL
BOLIVIA

Maderia River

Pôrto
Velho

R O N D Ô N I A

Ariquemes

BR-364

Jaru

Urueu-Wau-Wau
Reservation

Cacoal

Alvorado
do Oeste

BR-364

BR-429

Principe
da Beira

Vilhena

BRAZIL
BOLIVIA

EQUATOR

Amazon

RONDÔNIA

BRAZIL

Brasilia

BOLIVIA

São Paulo

SOUTH
AMERICA

settlers knowingly, or sometimes unknowingly, work land that is owned by big-business interests. When a business learns of this, it hires thugs to evict the settlers, often violently. Other settlers knowingly or unknowingly invade land that is "protected" as Indian reserves. Clashes between Indians and settlers or between Indians and loggers erupt. The clashes often involve knives or guns, and almost always the Indians are the losers. In 1988, for example, 14 unarmed men of the Tukuna tribe were massacred by gunmen hired by timber dealers. According to David Maybury-Lewis, of Cultural Survival, "cowboys turning jungle into ranches massacred sixteen Cuiva Indians in Colombia, including women and children. They escaped punishment by arguing in court that killing Indians was not considered a crime in the area. They were just 'animals, like deer or iguanas.' "

When the military rulers of Brazil started their colonization program in the early 1970s, they did so without any concern for Brazil's Indians. According to Gilio Brunelli, a member of a group trying to protect Brazil's Indian populations: "In 1950 there were as many as 35,000 known Indians in Rondônia, but now we think the population totals something like 5,000. For every Rondônian Indian there are 250 settlers. The Indians are dying off for many reasons, but mainly because of diseases brought in by outsiders." Disease combined with slave raids of old have wiped out 90 percent of Brazil's Indians. In the year 1500 there were six to nine million Brazilian Indians; today there are barely 200,000. The total number of tribes dropped from 230 in 1900 to about 120 in 1980. The major causes have been disease and starvation, not conflict. But conflict has taken lives as well, and it continues to do so today.

Brunelli is extremely critical of those who abuse Rondônia's Indians. Quoted in a *National Geographic* report, he said that "there were organized raids to kill Indians and get their lands. Whole villages have been wiped out. Members of the Zoro tribe, for example, were pushed around and killed by thugs from the town of J-Parana in order to consolidate land for one big rancher."

According to Cultural Survival, "The 700 or so Surui Indians of

Brazil were first 'officially' contacted in 1969. By 1974, half had died, mostly from influenza and measles. Although the Surui territory was marked in 1976 to establish its boundaries, the Surui's biggest problem has been the invasion of their lands by colonists. Colonists even illegally—and with immunity—constructed a road through the Surui lands."

Some of the Indian tribes, such as the Aroeira, regularly patrol their reserves to keep would-be intruders at bay. But some Indian reserves are so large that patrolling them is out of the question. The Tubarao/Latunde Indian reserve, for example, sprawls over 288,000 acres. Reserve or not, timber dealers, colonists, and in some cases the Indians themselves are cutting down the prime quality trees. There simply is no stopping such forest destruction.

Tribes that do enjoy government protection that sometimes is enforced, such as the Urueu-Wau-Wau tribe, are authorized to kill anyone who intrudes onto their land. And they do. The official population estimate of Urueu-Wau-Waus is 1,200, but the actual number may be closer to 350. Since the 1960s there have been some 45 Indian attacks on settlers and loggers. In 1979 Urueu-Wau-Waus killed two children of a settler and kidnapped another. (The settler was clearing Indian land that was mistakenly given to him by the federal government.) The only official contact such tribes have with the outside world is through medical aid stations set up for them and operated by the government. Measles, pneumonia, and influenza are common causes of Urueu-Wau-Wau deaths, especially among children. Even the common cold can have disastrous effects on the Urueu-Wau-Wau and other tribal people whose immune systems have not been conditioned by exposure to such ailments. And death from snakebite is not unusual among people of the forest.

Unofficial encounters with people from the outside world, including missionaries and anthropologists, are increasingly common. The missionary wants to change the Indians' way of life, but the anthropologist wants to study it before their cultures become so diluted by contact with the outside world that they are no longer unique. Each time an Indian visits the outside world or is visited by someone from that world, a little of his independence and freedom is lost. As one observer put it, "an integrated Indian is no longer an Indian but just a lesser citizen of the Brazilian nation."

Anthropologists sometimes come armed not only with their notebooks but with T-shirts, shorts, fishhooks, axes and machetes, kitchen pots, baseball caps, and mouth organs. As a number of scholars have learned, "once hooked on steel, the Indian cannot do without it."

At a settlement named Bom Futuro tens of thousands of miners shovel soil of the forest floor into water-filled troughs to wash out rich deposits of tin ore. The site was discovered in 1987 and has become filled with a rough-and-tumble collection of thugs and thieves mixed in with the miners. Gunfire starts at sunset and continues until dawn. Police have attempted to disarm the unruly miners but continually fail to find the guns, which the miners bury in plastic bags. Victims of nightly shoot-outs are discovered and highlighted in shafts of early morning sunlight. In 1988 the miners' shovels began to turn the soil of the Urueu-Wau-Wau's reserve, degrading the forest floor into knee-deep muck. All the Urueu-Wau-Wau can do is look on in anger. Their arrows and spears are no match for a thousand guns. Meanwhile, Indian children who visit the miners return shouting newly learned obscenities in Portuguese and wearing T-shirts with dirty words misspelled in English.

Garimpeiros they are called. They are the grizzled gold prospectors inching their way onto the land of Brazil's Yanomama Indians. According to one Yanomama, the miners "put poison in the water and the fish die." Another adds that "where the *garimpeiros* go, the Yanomama die."

The Asurinis Indians live between the Xingu and Ipiacava rivers in Rondônia. Like many other small tribes, all they can do is stand by and watch as colonists destroy their land. According to the anthropologist Berta Ribeiro, of the 53 Asurinis left, none wants more children. They know they are finished.

Whose Land Is It?

"Land" is the magic word in the vocabulary of any forest tribe. For Indians, the land that provides them with shelter, sustenance, protection, and privacy has a value far beyond the fulfillment of those needs—it has spiritual value. Once they feel that the sacredness of their land has been violated by the intrusion of miners, loggers, or others, the Indians feel a deep personal and group loss that humiliates them. What follows, usually, is one of two things. The Indians may try to defend their land against the intruders, which rarely works because the intruders have political clout, modern weapons and outnumber the Indians. Or, they agree to be absorbed into the overwhelming culture. The result of the latter is the loss of identity and dignity. The Indians become peasants without land ownership, laborers for those who took over their land, or beggars.

Respect, reverence, and love of the land is not easily understood by those who have never lived close to the land. For centuries the forest provided a home for the Conibo Indians. But recently logging interests took over their ancestral lands and cut down the forest. The Conibo have been reduced to working in lowly positions for the loggers.

Some countries look after their forest people. Others don't. Some pass laws that protect the Indians and their land. Others pass laws and then either ignore them or pass additional laws that contradict the protective ones. There are international agreements designed to protect the rights of tribal peoples, but most of the agreements are as vague as a painting done by a chimpanzee. New Zealand and Papua New Guinea have the best laws and the best enforcement of those laws to protect the land rights of their aboriginal tribes. An astonishing 97 percent of the land in Papua New Guinea is owned by its native tribes or clans. Individuals do not own the land; the tribes, as groups of individuals, own it.

Some countries, such as Peru, protect the land in the name of forest-dwelling tribes, but at the same time permit companies to move onto the "protected" land to drill for oil, gas, or other minerals. The tribes on the exploited land never receive a penny of the profits made on the oil, gas, or other minerals. Other South American countries, such as Bolivia, do not give their native forest tribes any right to their ancestral lands. Bolivia did sign an international agreement designed to provide such rights, but unfortunately, governments often pass laws to protect their native Indian populations and then ignore the laws.

One of the most heartless examples of such a practice was carried out by President Marcos of the Philippines. Although the Philippines had laws assuring tribal groups rights over their ancestral lands, Marcos laid down a contradictory law in 1974 that gave his government the right to use or abuse Indian ancestral lands any way the government wanted to. The law was called Presidential Decree 410.

Less than two weeks after Marcos announced Presidential Decree 410, the government licensed two logging companies to cut half a million acres of forest, much of which was part of the ancestral land of the Tinggian Indians in the province of Abra. For centuries the Tinggians lived on game and fish from the forest and maintained terraced and irrigated rice fields. The area marked for logging also invaded the land of four other tribes and four watersheds. One of the logging companies was owned by a relative of Imelda Marcos, the president's wife. And Marcos himself was said to have had a financial interest in the company.

In 1978 the Tinggians asked the government to stop floating logs down the river because the logs were damaging their fish traps and irrigation canals. They also asked that trees not be cut along creeks and watersheds to avoid erosion, and that certain forest areas be saved. The government said no to all requests. Furthermore, it told the Tinggians that they were "squatters," that they had no legal rights, and that some of them would have to move.

The following year the Tinggians tried again. This time 180 tribal leaders appealed to Marcos in writing: "We the people . . . are poor. All we have now are the mountains, trees, rivers, and especially our freedom. All these the [loggers are] threatening to take away from us."

Marcos responded by sending army troops into the area to prevent the Tinggians from holding mass meetings. The situation was made even worse when the World Bank, an international economic development organization, stepped in. It said it would finance an experimental forestry plantation on land held by the Tinggians. Most of the Tinggians in the area would have to move away. Some, however, could stay and work on the plantation. Workers would be given a quarter-acre plot as farmland, but they could keep it only while they worked for the plantation.

The World Bank's involvement is hard to understand, because the organization has a policy stating that it "will not assist development projects, forestry or otherwise, that knowingly encroach on traditional territories of tribal people without their full and voluntary consent." But this is not the only example of the World Bank's engagement in such destructive acts in the name of "development," as we noted in the previous chapter.

For many Tinggians in the areas of tree plantations, life is grim. They have lost the means of supporting themselves and helplessly watch the logging company degrade the land over widespread areas. Such destruction is also depriving Borneo's Penan of self-sufficiency. They used to be able to find game for food in three hours of hunting. Today they hunt for days and find nothing.

Although the well-being of many Indian groups living in tropical rain forests is being destroyed or seriously threatened, a few have organized themselves and fought back. We will discuss two such groups in Chapter 9, which describes ways in which we may save at least some of the remaining tropical rain forests.

In this chapter we have had a glimpse of how the destruction of rain forests is affecting the lives of people who make the forests their home. In the next we will turn our attention to ways in which ecologists are trying to learn about the forests as a vast integrated organism.

3
LEARNING ABOUT RAIN FORESTS

Remote and inhospitable, the world's tropical rain forests have been among the last patches of our planet to be explored scientifically. The industrial exploiters got to them long before organized scientific expeditions. However, some important scientific work was done in the 1800s. Among the earliest studies was a book containing many splendid drawings by German botanist C. F. P. von Martius who visited Amazonia from 1817 to 1820. For about 400 years after Columbus's first view of a tropical rain forest, scientists lacked a specific name for these forests.

English-speaking people loosely referred to tropical rain forests as jungles, and the French term *forêt* was equally vague. German botanist A. F. W. Schimper was the first, in 1898, to come up with a precise term for the tropical rain forest—*der tropische Regenwald*. He defined such forests as "evergreen, growing in wet places, at least 100 feet high, but usually much higher, rich in thick-stemmed lianas and in woody as well as herbaceous epiphytes [non-woody vines]." One of the most recent comprehensive books on rain forests was written by P. W. Richards. With the title *The Tropical Rain Forest*, it appeared in 1952. It was Richards who first used profile diagrams to show various aspects of a

Botanists draw "profile diagrams" to show the structure of a plot of forest veg-etation. A scale drawing of all plant types represented in the forest strip is made on graph paper. The same plot may be profiled at monthly or yearly intervals. Photographs often are taken in addition. Plant samples of each vegetation type in the profile also are collected for identification.

rain forest. Today scientists recognize 35 or more classes of rain forests, depending on their location, climate, tree types, and so on. Despite the many terms we use to distinguish between different kinds of rain for-ests, we are just beginning to learn about the many and intricate plant-animal relationships that make a tropical rain forest such a complex and fragile ecosystem.

How to Explore the Canopy

The canopy consists of the upper tiers of a tropical rain forest and is a fascinating world of intricate plant-animal associations. We know about some of them (See Chapter 5) but have hardly scratched the surface in our task of compiling a catalog. Most of the action in a tropical rain forest takes place not on the forest floor but up in the canopy at the height of a ten-story building.

One way to study life in the canopy is to climb a tree and poke around as you climb higher. This can be rewarding, but it also can be dangerous and sometimes frightening work. You can fall out of the tree, accidentally put your hand on a snake instead of a limb, stick your nose in a wasp's nest, or find yourself wallpapered with large stinging ants.

Another technique is to build a tree house, live in it for several weeks or months, and make observations. One such elevated observation post was built by the biologist M. Leighton 128 feet above the ground in a Borneo forest. To get to his platform he climbed a nylon rope ladder with rungs of wood. He spent most of his first night aloft

Strolling through the forest canopy on a specially constructed walkway, ecologist A. Mitchell studied a Panama forest around 1980. Highest point was an observation platform (e) about 130 feet above the forest floor. Mitchell could be raised in a chair lift (f), collecting samples along the way, from the base hut (g). A trap for catching bats (d) hangs from the walkway, which leads to a sleeping platform (c). Lighted traps (b) to attract and catch insects by night hang from a line by pulleys and are powered by electrical generators (a).

swatting mosquitoes rather than making observations, because at night the mosquitoes prowl that part of the forest where the warm-blooded animals live. Leighton had noticed few mosquitoes at night in his camp on the ground, where relatively few warm-blooded animals live.

From 1960 to 1969 the ornithologist H. E. McClure made observations from a tree house 190 feet above the forest floor in Malaya. Each week he noted when certain plants came into flower and bore fruit, and what the weather conditions were. He also identified and counted canopy birds, monkeys, squirrels, bats, and other critters.

Other tropical rain forest observers have expanded the idea of a tree house and built elaborate walkways. The investigators can then move through the canopy horizontally as well as vertically. Such walkways have been built in the forests of Panama, Papua New Guinea, and Sulawesi as part of "Operation Drake," carried out by A. Mitchell in 1981. The diagram shows how Mitchell studied animal life in the canopy.

Exploring by Canoe

Biologist E. J. H. Corner happened to be in Malaya in 1978 when a swamp forest was flooded. At such times trees may drown, lose their leaves, and begin to alter the canopy. If the flooding is only temporary the forest will be little changed, and the flood will provide a grand opportunity to paddle through the forest by boat and make unique observations. Here is how Corner described his canoe trip through a flooded forest:

"During the three days at Danau we paddled in a canoe through the flooded forest. . . . I could stand up at a height of twenty feet above the floor of the forest and collect from the tops of the undergrowth trees. Wherever we touched leaf, twig, trunk, or floating log, showers of insects tumbled into the canoe. Everything that could had climbed above the water. Ants ran over everything. I bailed insects and spiders instead of water, even scorpions, centipedes, and frogs. All around there was the incessant swishing of the half-submerged leaves, the oblong-lanceolate form of which was eminently successful for the occasion, and the incessant honking of frogs and toads. Lizards clung to the trunks; earthworms wriggled in the water, with snapping fish.

"I realized the importance of the hillocks in and around the swamp forest to animal life, for anything that could escape the flood must have fled there. We met no corpses. Pig, deer, tapir, rat, porcupine, leopard, tiger, monitor lizard, and snakes must have congregated on those hillocks in disquieting proximity."

Tracking the movements of animals by attaching radio transmitters to them is a valuable way to learn about the range of large mammals and to study their daytime and nighttime habits. It also enables field biologists to track the forced movements of animals displaced by the invasion of loggers, settlers, or miners. Such tracking reveals how large an area of forest is needed to support a single large mammal or a troop of monkeys, for instance. Miniature transmitters small enough to be implanted in a seed have been devised to trace the travels of certain large seeds.

Observing from the Air and Space

Photographs taken from airplanes, balloons, gliders, helicopters, and satellites are providing important information about the structure and composition of tropical rain forests. For example, in 1978 French researchers in a balloon made low passes of 2,600 feet and 820 feet above the canopy and took color photographs looking straight down. Since such photographs clearly make individual trees and small plots recognizable, they can be used to monitor changes over time. Fixed-wing aircraft and helicopters can accomplish the same thing. When pairs of such photos are made in a certain way, they can be viewed through special devices that produce clear, three-dimensional images of the forest. Even changes in soil texture and composition can be detected. Such monitoring by air is fast and easy, whereas ground parties have to climb through tangled forest, often over very difficult terrain.

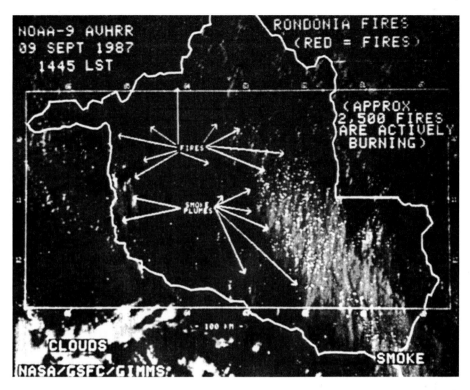

This satellite image generated from data collected by a weather satellite shows some 2,500 forest fires burning in the state of Rondônia, Brazil. The fires are set by small farmers and corporate ranchers to clear space for farming and grazing. Fast food hamburger outlets in the United States are among the major benefactors of such wholesale tropical rain forest destruction.

The ultimate tree house was designed by French architect Gilles Ebersolt. It is an enormous "raft" made of fiber netting supported by a six-sided frame of giant, hot-dog-shaped inflatable rubber tubes held together by six spokelike inflatable rubber struts. The raft is the size of a baseball diamond. A lighter-than-air balloon lifts and then carries the raft and its scientists over the forest, lowering onto a section of canopy the scientists want to study. The raft can be moved about from one section of canopy to another as often as the scientists call on their balloon taxi.

In 1989 French researcher Francis Halle lived for a year on his canopy raft studying a section of rain forest canopy in French Guiana, on the northeast coast of South America. He said that when the wind blew it was just like being on a huge rubber raft at sea, and at night, as the canopy released moisture through leaf transpiration, it was so wet that it seemed to rain *up*!

Satellite photographs, taken from altitudes of about 550 miles, reveal the forest landscape in remarkable detail. When magnified, these photos show objects more than 260 feet apart. Features such as logging roads and rivers appear as thin ribbons, and recent clearings stand out brightly from the darker surrounding forest. Satellite photographs are especially valuable in monitoring tropical forests on a global scale. They can be made frequently and so disclose instantly where illegal logging operations are being carried out, and where unwanted or illegal slash-and-burn activity is occurring. GEMS (Global Environment Monitoring System), developed by the United Nations in the late 1970s, is proving to be a valuable means of spotting the world's troubled forest areas.

Biomapping a Forest

One of the most important questions tropical rain forest ecologists must ask is "What have I left out of my study?" A forest's many parts—soil, plants, large animals, insects, weather—must be studied together and then viewed as a complex, single living system that is ever changing in response to itself and to outside forces imposed on it. No individual specialist, such as the soils scientist, botanist, or animal behaviorist, can see the entire picture. That view is at best fuzzy for the specialist and is only somewhat less fuzzy for the ecologist, who by education and training is geared to approach, if not attain, the grand view.

Cataloging the plant and animal species of a forest is known as biomapping the forest. It is an especially difficult job in a tropical rain forest because of the large numbers of animals and plants. But that is exactly the task a group of 280 scientists of Brazil's National Research Institute for Amazonia have set themselves. Their goal is to study key tropical forest areas so that they can draw up a master plan for "sustainable development," developing certain areas while preserving certain others. As an example of the difficulty of their goal, botanists examining a section of Brazilian rain forest near Manaus counted 1,652 species of trees and plants, 100 species of which had never been identified. According to botanist David Neill of the Missouri Botanical Garden, a few dozen acres of the Jatun Sacha section of Amazonian forest contain more tree species than all of the land in the United States east of the Mississippi.

As worldwide awareness and concern for tropical rain forests grow, a number of nations are providing support for scientific research in the Amazon. Among the leading nations are the United States, Great Britain, and Germany. The National Science Foundation of the United States also has offered to help by training researchers in conservation biology and restoration ecology.

While tropical rain forests are rich in species, we have far too few scientific specialists to study them. Probably there are fewer than 5,000 scientists worldwide who are knowledgeable about tropical ecosystems. Half that number specialize in identifying tropical forest species and know relatively little about the forests as a whole. One such expert in plant identification is Peter Raven of the Missouri Botanical Garden, one of the world's leading research centers in tropical forest study. Raven is troubled by the rapid pace of deforestation, which each year gobbles up an area about the size of Ohio. He says that during the next 25 years or so deforestation will wipe out about one million species. "No extinction episode of this magnitude has occurred during the past 65 million years," he says, "and the great majority of these species— and their potential for humanity—will disappear unknown."

Tropical rain forest ecology is a new field crying for scientific expertise. According to Raven, who is past chairman of the National Research Council's Committee on Research Priorities in Tropical Biology, "worldwide [in 1985], the total of scientists competent to undertake studies [to supervise and undertake large-scale projects in tropical ecological systems involving experimental modification] amounted to no more than two dozen."

Reliable information about the world's tropical rain forests is equally scarce. According to a 1988 report of the Worldwatch Institute, "despite growing recognition of the importance of forests to the economic and ecological health of nations, surprisingly little is known with certainty about the state of forest resources today. Many countries have not fully inventoried their forests, and the data that do exist vary widely in quality. In 1981, the United Nations Food and Agriculture Organization (FAO) generated the first global assessment of tropical forests that reconciled all data to a standard classification scheme and a standard base year. This study, which included correspondence with seventy-six countries and selective use of satellite imagery, still provides the best information available on tropical forests, even though much of the data are more than a decade old."

To show how quickly such information can become outdated, the 1981 United Nations study estimated that each year some 28 million acres of tropical forest are destroyed. A 1990 report by the World Resources Institute revised the figure to between forty and fifty million acres.

Considering the rapid rate at which the world's tropical rain forests are being plundered and are disappearing, studying them for their global importance is a race against time.

4
DIVERSITY
IN A
RAIN FOREST

Tropical rain forests are the planet's oldest, richest, and most diverse biological communities. Evolution has been playing out its grand experiments among the branches of many of these forests for tens of millions of years. For example, plants evolve poisonous chemical defenses as protection against leaf-eating insects. And the new defenses work, for a while at least. Then the insects evolve a new digestive chemistry that defeats the plants' defenses. Adaptation is a species's key to success, demonstrating how well the species is in tune with its environment and how well it may cope with environmental change.

Diversity Galore

South America's three-toed sloth is not a good house pet. It has become so specialized for life in the forest canopy—hanging from branches by its huge, hooked claws—that it can barely walk on the ground. The sloth is what biologists call a specialist. So are euglossine bees. They are so in tune with the flowers they visit to collect pollen that their wings beat to a frequency that triggers the flowers to conveniently release bursts of pollen.

The strangler fig does what its name implies. It begins as an epiphyte vine, a long-legged plant that wraps itself around a tree's branches and trunk and uses the tree for support only. For a while at least. Eventually the epiphyte develops roots that reach down to the ground, take hold, and compete with the roots of its support tree for nutrients. Meanwhile, the body of the strangler entwines the host tree, over the years covering the entire trunk of the tree. By this time the strangler's roots have become more efficient at taking up nutrients than are the roots of its host tree. Gradually the host tree dies and secretly rots away. In its place is the healthy strangler that has become a self-sufficient hollow "tree."

So many and so varied are the designs and behaviors of a tropical rain forest's plant and animal communities, and so bewildering their infinite interactions, that biologists who study the forests feel overwhelmed. Millions of species make up the world's tropical rain forests. More woody plant species grow on one forested volcano in the Philippines than occur in the United States from the Atlantic to the Pacific. Turn up ten square feet of tropical rain forest leaf litter and fifty species of ants come scurrying out. Shake a tree and about 1,700 insect species come raining down. For every human being there are three-quarters of a ton of termites worldwide. That may not seem surprising when you realize that termites have been around for 100 million years. Some scientists suspect that an estimate of 30 million tropical rain forest insect species may be low!

Amazonia has 1,171 known bird species. At least it did when this was written, but there are more. Brazil has 1,383 known fish species, but there are more. Central America has 456 fish species, but there are more. Compare those numbers with the total of 192 fish species in all of Europe and only 172 in the Great Lakes. Species of insects, let alone their individual numbers, are countless. They whir, whine, hum, and buzz with a million different voices.

The diversity just among the palm trees of South American rain forests is staggering—a total of 837 species. During his travels through these forests, Wallace was astounded by the Indians' knowledge and resourceful use of the wide variety of palms. The following account is from his book, *Palm Trees of the Amazon,* published in 1853.

"Suppose then we visit an Indian cottage on the banks of the Rio Negro, a great tributary of the river Amazon. . . . The main supports of the building are trunks of some forest tree of heavy and durable wood, but the light rafters overhead are formed by the straight cylindrical and uniform stems of the Jara palm. The roof is thatched with large triangular leaves, neatly arranged in regular alternate rows, and bound to the rafters with *sipos,* or forest creepers; the leaves are those of the carana palm. The door of the house is a framework of thin hard strips of wood neatly thatched over; it is made of the split stems of the Pashiuba palm.

"In one corner stands a heavy harpoon for catching the cowfish; it is formed of the black wood of the Pashiuba barriguda. By its side is a blowpipe ten or twelve feet long, and a little quiver full of small poisoned arrows hangs up near it. . . . it is from the stem and spines of two species of palms that they are made. His great bassoon-like musical instruments are made of palm stems; the cloth in which he wraps his most valued feather ornaments is a fibrous palm spathe, and the rude chest in which he keeps his treasures is woven from palm leaves. His hammock, his bow-string and his fishing-line are from the Tucum. The comb which he wears on his head is ingeniously constructed of the hard bark of a palm, and he makes fish hooks of the spines, or uses them to puncture on his skin the peculiar markings of his tribe.

"His children are eating the agreeable red and yellow fruit of the Pupunha or peach palm, and from that of the Assai he has prepared a favourite drink, which he offers you to taste. That carefully suspended gourd contains oil, which he has extracted from the fruit of another species; and that long, elastic, plaited cylinder used for squeezing dry the mandioca pulp to make his bread, is made of the bark of one of the singular climbing palms, which alone can resist for a considerable time the action of the poisonous juice. In each of these cases a species is selected better adapted than the rest for the peculiar purpose to which it is applied, and often having several different uses which no other plant can serve as well, so that some little idea may be formed of how important to the South American Indian must be these noble trees, which supply so many daily wants, giving him his house, his food, and his weapons." Wallace mentioned 15 palm species.

Giants and Species Spacing

The tropical rain forests are also the home of giants: slugs eight inches long, giant snails, spiders that eat birds, trees with six-foot-long leaves, bees the size of hummingbirds, beetles the size of a child's fist, and butterflies with ten-inch wing spans, so large that children tie strings to them and lead them dancing through the air. In the evening girls put fireflies in their hair to make it sparkle.

Because so many plant species occupy a relatively small space, few individuals of the same species grow on a plot of several acres—competition would be overwhelming. Sometimes there are as few as one small plant or one tree of a given species per acre. Wallace observed this single-species scarcity and commented that one could search in all directions and fail to find another tree of the kind just observed until walking half a mile or more. Although about 400 species of trees grow on a fifty-seven-acre patch of Malaysian rain forest, 160 of them occur only once. Spotty distribution is an adaptation that protects a species— disease and parasites could thrive if many individuals of the same species grew so close together that their branches and leaves intermingled. For good reason, disease and insect pest problems are rare in mixed tropical rain forests.

German botanist Marius Jacobs points out that "a small population density also implies more space and opportunities for other species." Further, seeds may have a better chance of surviving if they are deposited relatively far from their parent tree. This would be the case when seed-eating insects and birds congregate about a cluster of the same kinds of trees to feed when the trees bear fruit. After the feast there would be few if any seed-bearing fruits left to germinate and become new trees. A seed's chances of survival probably are increased if the seed has some way of being carried some distance away from such an area of mass feeding, by a bird or some other animal, and deposited far from home.

When *very* many plants of the same species grow closely together, an opposite event may occur. The mother plant may swamp consumers with so many seeds at one time that some are always left over—enough to keep the tree population vigorous. You might wonder how the trees of a tropical rain forest are pollinated, since two trees of any one species usually are so far apart. In an open hardwood forest, pollen is carried on the wind and distributed throughout the forest. Because wind is rare in a tropical rain forest, evolution's infinite contest of trial and error has seen to it that pollination is carried out by bats, birds, insects, and other animals—an essential zoological link with the plant world. In central Europe's open forests about 20 percent of the plants depend on the wind for pollination. Among 760 plant species studied in Borneo's Brunei tropical forest, the only species that was found to be wind-pollinated grew on mountain ridges exposed to rising air currents.

Although wide dispersion of a single species in a tropical rain forest seems to be an advantageous adaptation, there is a minus side. A widely dispersed species may be at greater risk of extinction than a safety-in-numbers species. This is one of many examples of the fragility of a tropical rain forest. But it is the course evolution has directed.

Evolution: A Broad View

On one level we can regard "life" as an activity, or process, of the right mix of chemicals reacting with the environment. That right mix might be in the form of an owl, a mosquito, or a single cell, such as an amoeba. Each has those characteristics we collectively call "life." They include:

1. the ability to protect itself within a membrane that acts as a defense against the disorderly outside world;

2. a process, involving energy, that drives the many chemical activities that make new parts, repair worn or damaged parts, and gen-

AMOEBA

false foot

nucleus
food sac
waste fluids sac

An amoeba is an independent cell that carries out all life functions. It is a mass of protoplasm contained within a cell membrane that stretches this way and that. To move, the amoeba simply flows into a bulge in its cell membrane, called a "false foot." It engulfs food particles, then stores and "eats" them in food sacs called food vacuoles. Its fluid wastes collect in fluid vacuoles that exit the cell by passing through the cell membrane.

erally maintain the organism from one minute to the next;

3. a way of obtaining matter and energy from the outside environment and using that matter and energy for growth and maintenance; and

4. a way of reproducing more organisms like itself.

All organisms of the same makeup and general behavior, such as dogs, cats, palm trees, or people, belong to a certain species. Human beings belong to the species *Homo sapiens*, cats to the species *Felis domesticus*, and the tropical rain forest's ironwood trees to the species *Eusideroxylon zwageri*. We can define a species as any population whose individual members look pretty much alike, who mate and produce offspring, and whose offspring in turn can have offspring. Over long periods of time a species may change, or evolve, into a new species. Or all members of a species may die, in which case the species becomes extinct. That is what happened to the many species of dinosaurs some

65 million years ago. Of all the species of animals and plants that have ever lived on Earth, 99.99 percent are now extinct. However, life itself has continued uninterrupted as new species have evolved and replaced the ones that became extinct.

Sometimes extinctions occur quietly and go unnoticed, as is happening in the tropical rain forests today. Other times they are catastrophic. Several single catastrophic events have shaken Earth in the past, and each has wiped out at least 95 percent of all living species. That is an impressive figure when you consider the millions of species that exist at a given moment.

When scientists study the ways in which living matter has evolved since it first appeared on Earth nearly four billion years ago, they examine life on many different levels—on the level of cells, on the level of whole organisms, whether a tree or a turtle, on the level of populations of those organisms, and on the level of communities of mixed populations of organisms and how they affect each other.

Biological evolution on the scale that has occurred on Earth needs a lot of time. It is impossible for the mind to grasp the meaning of a

Similarity in structure among related groups of animals (here, the primates) is persuasive evidence that they evolved from a common ancestor. Long claws in tree shrews evolved into nails in monkeys, apes, and humans. Notice the similarity in the finger pads of lemurs and tarsiers. The hands of all six primates are specialized for grasping.

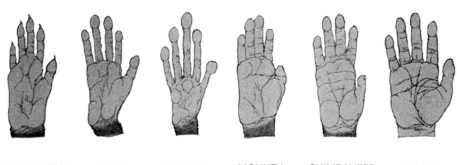

TREE SHREW   LEMUR   TARSIER   MONKEY   CHIMPANZEE   HUMAN

million or a billion years of evolution. If it helps, let each page of this book represent one year. A billion years would be represented by a stack of these books (without their covers) about fifty miles high.

Not only did biological evolution need a long time to give rise to the astonishing assortment of plants and animals known to us past and present, but just the right conditions on our planet also were needed for the process of chemical and biological evolution to begin—the right kinds of chemical raw materials, the right environmental conditions, and energy to manipulate that matter. Those conditions existed in the distant past, and the process of organic evolution continues to operate today. It occurs all around us, and its pace quickens in tropical rain forests.

The Pace of Evolution

The age of many tropical rain forests, tens of millions of years, is one reason why they are so diverse. Another is the pace of evolution there. Among the richest of the older forests are those of Southeast Asia, which contain "living fossils" such as the ginkgo tree, a relic of the evolutionary past that has changed hardly at all over the millennia. The most ancient pollen grains botanists have found in Borneo are about 30 million years old, which probably dates the age of the forest itself. Those regions that have undergone long periods of drying, such as West Africa, can claim only small diversity by contrast.

One of the driving forces of evolution is environmental upheaval, such as the formation of a vast river that cuts a forest in two, or the upthrust of a new mountain range that splits an environmental setting in two. Any such geologic change that divides a population of a given species and then isolates the fragmented populations from each other is a spur to evolution. As a result of the geologic change, environmental conditions on each side of the river or mountain range may become different in small but significant ways. As each fragmented population responds to changes in its environment, it may evolve into a new species. Let's see how this works on the level of genes and gene pools.

The Carboniferous period, some 300 million years ago, was a warm period that favored lush vegetation growth and the formation of swamps. Dead and dying plants, including numerous fern species, littered the swamp waters, were compressed, and eventually turned into peat, the first stage in the formation of coal.

Evolution at Work

How well a population of palm trees or cockroaches responds to a change in its environment depends on genetic variation among the individuals making up the population. Variation expresses itself in many ways—the ability of a plant to go without water for a long time, how well a tree competes for nutrients with a neighboring tree, how swift or clever an animal is in escaping predators. Each member of the population has abilities and weaknesses that differ from the abilities and weaknesses of every other member of the population.

If, for instance, the climate turns unusually warm, those individuals that can withstand the temperature rise survive, and those that can't withstand the heat die. Those that survive pass their "heat-survival" genes on to their offspring and into the population's gene pool. Gradually the population changes as the less fit are weeded out by their inability to tolerate the temperature change and the individuals with "heat-survival" genes increase their numbers. Through just such beneficial changes in the gene pool, a population adapts to changes in its environment. When the gene pools of two fragmented populations have changed to the extent that individuals of the two populations can no longer mate and produce offspring, species change through evolution has taken place. It is not individuals that evolve, but populations. It may take 50,000 years for a new species to evolve, but there is no fixed time.

Evolution, then, is expressed as those changes in a population's gene pool that make the population ever better adapted to its environment. In addition to favoring genes that are beneficial and make a population more fit, evolution at the same time tends to weed out from the gene pool those individuals whose genes are harmful to the population. The process of nature selecting fitter individuals for survival and weeding the less fit out of the population is called natural selection.

Natural selection, and hence evolution, is speeded along in tropical rain forests where there are no interruptions in the growing season and, in many instances, in the breeding season. All year long there is continuous transportation of genetic material. Temperatures that are relatively high and stay that way tend to speed along not only the rate of growth but also the rate at which new individuals develop from young into adults. For instance, individuals of an insect species living in a temperate environment may require several months to complete their life cycle. Members of a similar species in a tropical environment may require only a few weeks.

Another reason why the pace of evolution is quickened in a tropical rain forest is that nooks and crannies that provide myriad ecological opportunities for evolution to explore and experiment with are nearly limitless. The sheer abundance of life offers evolution infinite possibilities. New species of animals tend to evolve more rapidly than new species of plants. There are several reasons. Generally plants cannot produce a new and mature generation of individuals as quickly as animals can. The large tree species live anywhere from 100 to 500 or more years. But our knowledge about longevity among large tropical rain forest trees is poor because the forests have not been studied for very long. Also, because the trees grow all year they do not produce annual growth rings, which are generally reliable age tags for trees in seasonal forests. So it is hard to determine the age of a tropical rain forest tree, or to estimate its life span. We do know that it takes the dipterocarp tree 50 to 60 years to come into flower. By comparison, a female orangutan produces a new generation in only ten years.

Another reason why the pace of evolution is slower for tropical forest plants than for animals is that the plants stay put and depend largely on animal agents to disperse their seeds over areas of new habitats. In contrast, animals move about and continuously investigate the suitability of various habitats. This difference in the pace of evolution explains why there are usually many more animal species than plant species. It may take rain forest plants at least 50 generations to evolve a new species when conditions for new species formations are at their best. But short-lived plants may require 250,000 generations!

The amount of time that evolution needs for experimentation can be appreciated when we understand the idea of "mutual avoidance." One group of ants living on the underside of leaves conveniently avoids the group living on the top surface of the leaves. Birds may occupy one level of the canopy by day, but by night bats become active and use the space. Mutual avoidance is the key to success in sharing the same ecological niche. The evolution of such thriving associations of different species sharing the same niche does not come about overnight. Usually millions of years of trial and error are needed. But there has been both time and space for such experimentation. The larger the area of tropical rain forest, the more ecological niches there are. The greater the number of niches, the richer the evolutionary possibilities. And the richer the evolutionary possibilities, the greater the explosion of new species to produce and maintain biological diversity, or biodiversity. Biodiversity is the very lifeblood of success of tropical rain forests. Dilute it and the forest begins to die.

As we find out how a tropical rain forest is built, or structured, in the next chapter, we will see examples of biodiversity in action.

5

HOW A RAIN FOREST IS BUILT

In her insightful book about tropical rain forests, Catherine Caufield comments on the popular delusion that the average tropical rain forest has well-watered and extremely fertile soils. She cites the unrealistic impression of the young Alfred Wallace who in 1878 wrote of Amazonia: "When I consider the excessively small amount of labor required in this country to convert the virgin forest into green meadows and fertile plantations, I almost long to come over with half-a-dozen friends, disposed to work, and enjoy the country; and show the inhabitants how soon an earthly paradise might be created."

Although the soils of a tropical rain forest receive a lot of water, they are poor compared with the soil of a Nebraska or Ukraine wheat farm. On marveling over the dense and rich growth of a tropical rain forest, many Western visitors to those forests incorrectly concluded that the rich growth must mean rich soil for agriculture. If they browsed through a botany text they would learn that the rich growth in poor soil is a result of millions of years of evolution giving rise, through trial and error, to plants with the right kinds of genes. The right genetic makeup is the key to a species' ability to survive in an environment that other species find hostile. Adaptation is the biologist's term for species success in any environment.

Beneath the Forest Floor

If the soil of a tropical rain forest is so poor, how do the forest's many plant species survive? Just a few inches beneath the soil surface in any forest are billions of plant and animal organisms that form their own special webs of life with food chains and energy stores quite different from those in the airy forest above. Sunlight never reaches this underground community of living things, and thus they need a different source of energy. That source is the waste products and dead remains of the plants and animals above.

A leaf high in the canopy dies, detaches from its branch, zigzags gently down through the understory of low-growth plants, and comes to rest as a piece of litter on the damp forest floor. Were this a northern forest, the leaf could lie there for many months before the decomposers (bacteria and fungi) of the soil began to reduce it to humus, the broken-down organic matter that makes garden soil "rich," or fertile. But the high temperatures that favor rapid activity in a tropical rain forest begin the decay process almost immediately and carry it out quickly.

By acting on dead matter from above, soil organisms remove the last bit of energy from dead plant and animal tissue and change it into minerals, gases, and water, all of which can be used again and again. The soil is a huge stomach that digests virtually everything that happens to fall into it.

According to some estimates, a thimbleful of rich tropical soil contains about 1,004,225,000 organisms. About a billion are bacteria, which are among the smallest living things known to us. About another four million are organisms very much like bacteria. Some accomplish what no animal can do—digest wood.

Although termites may chew up your garage, they are unable to digest the wood they eat. The job is done by microbes (bacteria and protozoans) that live in the guts of the termites. By digesting the wood, they produce a sugarlike substance that is the termites' real food. While the microbes produce nourishment for the termites and for themselves, the termites in turn provide homes for their food suppliers.

The most important decomposers in all forest soils are not the bacteria but another group of organisms, the fungi. Dig up some forest soil and turn it over. You will probably find an endless tangle of gray-white threads. Follow them to their source and you will find a mass of them attached to a piece of dead leaf or branch. That gray-white network is that part of a fungus called *mycorrhizae*. Its threadlike strands give off a substance that breaks down the dead leaf into food that the fungus can use. The toadstools, puffballs, and mushrooms growing out of the forest floor are the reproductive parts of fungi. Fungi break

Decomposers, such as this shelf-fungus growing on a rotting tree trunk, are the chief agents of decay in forests. Dead plant and animal matter alike are broken down by decomposer fungi and bacteria into a rich supply of nutrients for the living. They liberate carbon, nitrogen, calcium, and other nutrients, which are returned to the soil for recycling.

down wood and break down and digest the hard bonelike shells of beetles and other insects. They are the garbage collectors of the soil. Fungi give off a substance that makes forest soil acid, a condition that favors them but favors bacteria less.

As an eat-and-be-eaten life goes on above the ground, one also goes on within the soil. Many organisms spend all or at least part of their time in the soil: earthworms, beetles, snails, slugs, mites, millipedes and centipedes, snowfleas, spiders, small white worms called pot worms, and much smaller wormlike animals called nematodes. The nematodes are usually too small to be seen without a microscope.

In addition to eating dead and dying matter, some fungi in the soil trap and digest live nematodes. One fungus traps by forming a loop made up of three cells. As a nematode unwittingly enters the loop and brushes against the cells, the cells swell to about three times their resting-stage size and squeeze the nematode in a death grip. The cells swell up in about one-tenth of a second. The fungus then digests the worm by sticking feeding threads into it.

The soil of the forest floor is home to more different kinds and a greater number of plant and animal organisms than any other part of the forest. The decomposers of the soil depend on a steady rain of dead plant and animal matter from above, and all living plants and animals ultimately depend on the soil for life-giving nutrients in the form of minerals. Although we can peel away a forest and examine it layer by layer, we must not lose sight of the forest as a whole. Only by seeing all of its many components working together can we understand what a forest is and what it does.

On the Forest Floor

Resting on top of the soil is a spongy mat containing embedded root hairs, bacteria, fungi, decaying twigs, tree limbs, the carcasses of dead insects, and other once-living material. The one-inch to two-inch layer of decomposing litter of a tropical rain forest floor rarely has a chance to grow thicker because the forest organisms need nutrients for growth and maintenance. The tiny root hairs invade a fallen leaf and speed the work of the decomposers. The leaf is soon mechanically and chemically broken down. In the process it releases nutrient elements on which all forest growth depends—nitrogen, calcium, potassium, phosphorus, and sodium.

Nutrient cycling in a tropical rain forest is the most efficient of any forest biome. As much as 99 percent of the nutrients released by the decaying litter on the floor may be reabsorbed by the fine and shallow roots of giant trees and small shrubs. Very few nutrients are lost to the forest by seepage of its ground water into streams and rivers. Tropical rain forests are called "closed systems" because they generate and regulate their nutrient resource, maintain their water budget, and control their own local climate.

The ability of a tree root to take up nutrients from the soil is increased by mycorrhizae, those beneficial fungus invaders that live as part of a tree's root system. When the nutrient phosphorus, for example, exists in amounts too small for a root to take up, the mycorrhizae go to work and take in the nutrient for the plant's use. "When the water pump stops working, use a sponge." The plant provides a safe place for the fungi to live; in exchange the fungi provide essential nourishment to the plant. This is only one of thousands of examples of two different organisms living together in mutual benefit. The term for such communal living is mutualism. In certain regions of a forest where the soil is low in nutrients, many trees that lack the mycorrhizae die. When a forest with low soil fertility is destroyed, and the mycorrhizae along with it, the forest is unable to grow again. Although they have tried, botanists have not been able to infect a large area of forest with mycorrhizae. The process must occur in its own way and at its own pace. This is only one example of how little we know about "managing" a forest or even helping a forest to manage itself.

Termites also play an important role in keeping a tropical rain forest floor picked clean of dead and dying twigs, fallen branches, and trees. Almost as fast as this dead matter falls to the ground, termites,

A large Brazilian tropical rain forest tree has many lower trunk structures called buttresses, which help support it and may help move nutrients up the trunk to the leaves. Buttresses occur on trees with weak and shallow roots, which grow mainly in tropical rain forests. The drawing, made by Martius between 1817 and 1820, was published in Flora Brasiliensis *in 1842.*

earthworms, ants, and other soil organisms carry bits and pieces of the litter down into the ground where they convert it into humus. But most of the decomposition of litter takes place on the forest floor, not beneath it, and therefore a tropical rain forest has a very limited humus budget. And that, in turn, is the reason for the soil's poor fertility, which Wallace and others before and after him failed to recognize.

Another myth about tropical rain forests is that they contribute significantly to the world's supply of free oxygen through the photosynthesis of their green leaves and stems. These forests have (mistakenly) been termed the "green lungs" of our planet, but in fact they tend to use up as much oxygen in the process of breaking down organic matter as they produce during photosynthesis. (To find out how photosynthesis works, see Explanation 2.)

Just as earthworms help churn up the soil by tunneling through it, so do termites and ants. As termites build their huge mound-nests, they make many tunnels that let air and water mix with the soil. Ants are just as numerous and live at all levels of the forest, from beneath the soil to the highest leaves in the canopy. While one species of ant may spend most of its time on the underside of leaves, another may use only the top surfaces. The economy of tropical rain forest life would put a Wall Street wizard to shame.

Beware the Army Ants

Among the more interesting of the tropical ants are the many species of army ants, extensively studied in the Canal Zone by the late T. C. Schneirla. Unlike termites that build elaborate mound-nests, army ants spend most of their time wandering about on extensive manuevers foraging for food. Some of their marauding packs number as many as twenty million, and it is a good idea to stay out of their way because they are meat eaters. Their chief foods are insects and worms, although they will consume a helpless bird or any large animal that has been crippled and stranded. They sting their victims to death and then pick them apart. The bits and pieces are brought back to their temporary nests to be shared with the rest of the colony.

The forced march of a troop of army ants usually begins in the morning in the bivouac area where many of the ants are protectively grouped around the queen and the young. Although the workers usually start out in one direction and follow a main trail, they soon fan out and form numerous branches that span a distance of twenty feet or more. Eventually the workers at the most forward positions begin to turn around, carrying food bits back to the colony. In a troop of several million ants, traffic jams sometimes build up as the returning ants follow the same chemical scent trails used by the foraging ants going in the opposite direction.

By the end of the day all of the ants have returned to the colony for the night. A colony stays in its temporary nest while the new brood of young ants is still in the pupal stage of development. But soon after the young ants emerge from their pupae and begin to move about, the entire colony packs up and troops off to a new location. It remains in the new area until the next brood of young emerge from their pupae.

Each troop of foraging army ants has camp followers—birds and other animals that eat insects. Among them are wild pigs, anteaters, and tapirs that use their long snouts to poke and upturn the soil to expose insects when the ground surface does not offer a ready meal. These and other animals of the forest floor usually are hard to see because of their coloring, which protects them against big cats or other large predators.

Life Zones from Floor to Canopy

The forest has several markedly different life zones, each with its unique associations of plant-animal communities and its own microclimate.

Moving upward from the tropical rain forest floor, the first thing you notice is the tangle of vines and other plants growing and hanging from the trunks and branches of the trees. Some, called lianas, have roots in the ground but grow up the tree stems and flower high above the forest floor in the canopy. Another group of plants, called epi-phytes, also grows among the trees of the understory and canopy. Unlike the lianas, most epiphytes do not root themselves in the ground, although some do. In this way they do not sap energy from the trees they grow on. They use the trees only for support. Orchids and other epiphytes soak up water from the moist air as blotting paper does, or they collect it in their cuplike leaves when it rains. Insects, including mosquitoes and water beetles, make their homes in these tiny leaf-pools. Some of the larger leaves catch and hold sizeable pools of water that become habitats for larger aquatic species, including frogs and salamanders. The dimly lighted floor of an African tropical rain forest is home for numerous animals. Among the large varieties are ele-phants, crocodiles, hogs, gorillas, and okapis. Butterflies and moths move silently through the heavy, humid air while beetles, snails, termites, ants, and shrews go about their business of eating and being eaten. Among the butterflies is one "invisible" variety with transparent wings.

Just above the ground in the understory are different species of beetles and butterflies, several species of frogs, squirrels, leopards, vipers, and pythons. From higher up come the shrieks of chimpanzees and several species of monkeys. Parrots, owls, butterflies, sunbirds, and eagles also make the canopy their condominium.

South American, Malaysian, and other of the world's tropical rain forests all have large animals and a host of varied plant-animal asso-ciations, some involving the large animals themselves. South America, for example, has jaguars, anacondas, tapirs, and giant armadillos, as well as its great sloths. The fur of the three-toed sloth may be home for a hundred or more parasites, including not only mites and ticks but beetles and moths as well. For protection against large predators, the sloths depend on a green camouflage "paint" that enables them to blend in with the green background of the forest. The disguise is provided by green algae that make their home in the sloth's fur. The numbers of parasite-host and other intricate plant-animal relationships in a tropical rain forest are limitless, as are the nooks and crannies occupied by insects and other forest critters.

Every inch of ground in the Hoh Rain Forest in Washington's Olympic National Park is carpeted with vegetation reflecting soft green light. The branches and trunks of older trees are draped with a profusion of mosslike plants called epiphytes. Although the epiphytes live off nutrients from the moist air, eventually these plants choke their host trees, killing them.

Many of the inhabitants of the forests in the countries just mentioned are different from those in an African or Central American
tropical rain forest. Bird species differ, for example, as do monkey
species.

Life in the Canopy

The topmost layer of the forest is the canopy. From the air it looks
like a great sprawling, soft, wavy blanket with patches of dark and light
here and there. The upper canopy of the forest is exposed to beating
rains and wind during a storm and is flooded in bright sunlight on a
cloudless day. Because the broad leaves of the upper canopy are thin,
sunlight passes through them and reaches the understory and forest
floor.

During a heavy rain the large drops beat the leaves, tipping them
this way and that and allowing other drops to fall past. Such storms
wet the entire forest, from upper canopy to soil. But during a light
rain the leaves of the upper canopy tend to collect the small raindrops
until there is enough water to trickle down the leaf stem into leaf-
pools, then flow along the branches, down the tree trunk, and sometimes into the ground around the base of the tree. This "leaffall" and
"stemfall" water carries nutrients that are deposited on the plant's
leaves and stems. However, much of the forest floor may remain relatively dry during a light rain.

Because the upper canopy is bathed in sunlight and open to air
movement, its air tends to be drier than the air lower down. Closer to
the forest floor the air is moister, being moistest at ground level. There
is little air movement just above the forest floor, and moisture given
off by the leaves tends to collect, hang in the air just above the floor,
and make the forest muggy. Without sunlight to evaporate some of
the moisture, the forest is especially muggy at night.

As the amount of moisture in the air changes from canopy to
forest floor, so does the temperature. By day, the air temperature of
the canopy and understory is higher than the air temperature just

above the ground. But at night the air temperature, like the amount of moisture, tends to be pretty much the same from canopy to ground. Soon after sunrise the daytime difference is felt again.

More animals live in the canopy than on the forest floor and in the understory combined. Because the canopy has few predators, birds need not fear calling attention to themselves by wearing extravagantly colored plumage. Among such kaleidoscopic birds are parakeets, birds of paradise, and toucans. Among the few predatory species of the canopy are snakes, South America's harpy eagle, and the Philippines' monkey-eating eagle. The canopy is also occupied by cockroaches, rats, and mice. In the penthouse of the forest, called the emergent layer, are woodpeckers, numerous insects, and leaping monkeys that use their plumed tails as rudders.

Orangutans are tree dwellers of the tropical rain forests of Sumatra and Borneo. These large red-haired apes spend most of their time high in the forest canopy where they feed and sleep in nests they make each night of branches and twigs. They enjoy a wide range of food— more than ninety different species of fruits and a dozen or more different kinds of leaves, sprouts, bark, and orchid bulbs. Their diet includes about 115 different plant species. Their broad diet enables them to find food all year, and their favorite food is eight different species of figs. Orangutans move easily through the forest roof exploring this or that fig tree for the desirable stage of fruit ripeness. They have learned to observe the flight patterns of birds known as hornbills, which also are fig eaters. If the apes see many hornbills flying off in one direction, they follow the birds. The reward? Trees with figs of just the right ripeness.

Ants and other insects are everywhere, from the ground to the highest twigs of the highest trees that stretch above the canopy. They are found hiding in the crevices of bark, trooping along branches, clinging to the edges of leaves, and living on larger animals that make the understory and canopy their home. Monkeys and other animals of the canopy are food for mosquitoes, the mosquitoes are food for bats and small birds, and the bats and small birds are food for owls and other large predatory birds. Many canopy species spend their entire lives in only one habitat level of the canopy, never leaving that zone. Rare are the individuals that habitually move back and forth between the understory to the canopy.

Plant-Animal Relationships

Some would use the word "outlandish" to describe nature's ingenuity in designing certain plant-animal relationships that enable survival through adaptaton. Consider, for example, the acacia thorn plant and the ants that live on it. The acacia has tender leaf tips that the ants cut off and use as food for their young. The ants chew a window opening near the tip of a thorn and use the interior as living quarters. So the plant provides the ants with both food and shelter. In return, the ants meet two essential needs of the acacia. They patrol the acacia day and night, biting and stinging insect invaders that attempt to use the plant as food. The acacia, unlike many other plants, lacks a chemical defense system to repel harmful insects. In addition to protection from insects, the acacia needs full sunlight for healthy growth. Whenever another plant grows too close to the acacia and threatens it with shade, the ants cut through the trespassing plant's soft stem and cut off its leaves. Deprived of acacia leaf tips, the ants would die. Deprived of the ants, the acacia would die.

With no means of active defense, numerous caterpillar species have evolved canny adaptations that protect them from being eaten by wasps, ants, and other predators. The Latin American caterpillar *Thisbe irenea*, for example, emits a syrupy fluid rich in sugar and amino acids. Ants, which otherwise would eat the soft-bodied caterpillars, eat the highly nutritious syrupy fluid instead. In return for their meal, the ants protect the caterpillars from wasps and other predators. *Thisbe irenea* calls its ant protectors for dinner by rubbing its bumpy head back and forth against two rod-shaped organs. The resulting high-pitched, rhythmic chirping sound is picked up by the ants, which come trooping to table. There are thousands more plant-insect relationships waiting to be discovered, such as a recently detected one that involves corn seedlings. Right after being chewed on by caterpillars, the young leaves of corn seedlings release large amounts of chemicals called terpenoids. A certain species of female wasp detects the terpenoids, flies to the injured leaf, and eats the caterpillar. So the seedling leaves tend to be protected from caterpillar pests. Interestingly, a corn seedling leaf that is damaged accidentally does not release terpenoids.

According to botanist Marius Jacobs, 22 of the 830 plants he collected from New Guinea lived in some kind of specialized association with ants. Many are the delicate balances between plants and animals in tropical rain forests.

Hollow Trees and Their Guests

A number of tropical rain forest trees have evolved hollow cores. This seemingly unusual state occurs when soils lack nutrients. Animals that use the hollow core for shelter deposit food and their body wastes inside the tree. Rich in nutrients, the wastes are absorbed into the ground where they are taken up by the tree's roots.

Tropical forest birds called hornbills would not be able to survive without these hollow trees. This association provides another example of an intricate evolutionary relationship between plants and animals. During the mating season, the female hornbill and her mate select a hollow tree and the female climbs inside for her breeding period. From the outside the male begins to block the entrance, leaving only a small opening. He uses a cementlike substance that contains rotting wood, soil, and other materials. Working from the inside, the female helps construct the plug. During the time the female lays her eggs and tends them, the male brings her food, stuffing it through the small opening. In her "prison," or sanctuary, the female, her eggs, and eventually the young hatchlings, remain safe from predators. When the enclosure becomes too small for both the female and her young, she breaks out with help from her mate. From the outside, both birds rebuild a shield to protect the young that remain inside; they feed the young through a small slit. This care continues until the offspring are ready to begin life on the outside.

Loggers have little use for hollow trees because the trees have no commercial value. As a result, the hollow trees are being deliberately destroyed to "improve" the forest. When deprived of its habitat and suitable breeding places, the hornbill fails to mate. The hornbills are fruit-eating birds and range widely over the forest canopy, thus dispersing a great many and a great variety of seeds far and wide throughout the forest. Whether it is in the scattering of seeds or in some other way, all animals of the tropical rain forest play some role or other in maintaining the forest's complex webs of life. For that reason we can regard a tropical rain forest, or any other forest, as a vast complex organism made up of many interrelated parts.

The Brazil-Nut Mystery

Caufield relates a story about Brazil nuts, the complete reproductive cycle of which remains a mystery. Brazil nuts usually are the last ones left in a Thanksgiving nut bowl because it's too much work to crack them open and pry out the meat. They are a rain forest product picked by Indians and peasant farmers from trees widely scattered across the forest.

Not a very efficient way to gather nuts, thought one enterprising businessman. So he started a plantation, planting lots of Brazil-nut trees close together in neat rows. The trees grew well and eventually flowered. But no nuts. When the businessman asked the experts why his trees didn't produce nuts, no one could tell him because no one knew how the flowers of a Brazil-nut tree are pollinated.

One part of the story was known, however. The males of a certain species of bee regularly visit Brazil-nut trees. It was also known that the bees are put into the condition to mate only when the chemicals of certain orchid species are available to them. The plantation had no such orchids, or other plant foods of the bees. Why Brazil nuts had for so long been gathered so "inefficiently" from trees scattered across the forest soon became clear. The life cycle of the trees involves a network of other plant-animal associations that exist only in a large mixed forest. To this day, no one has cracked the Brazil-nut case, except cat-sized rodents called agoutis. They seem to be the only ones with sharp enough teeth, and an appropriate appetite, to want to break through the hard outer case and expose the nut. The agoutis aren't telling the rest of the story.

Virtually all rain forest species depend on many other species to make a living. We are just now beginning to learn some of the laws that regulate tropical rain forest plant-animal associations, but the web of relationships is so tangled and so vast that we will never learn our way through all of it. What saddens many biologists is that the rain forests are being demolished so fast that they may never even have the chance to learn in detail how rain forests work, or even identify all the benefits the forests have to offer.

One reason why the near infinite number of plant-animal relationships have been able to survive is the tropical rain forest's virtually changeless climate. Plant-animal relationships tend to be stable and "permanent" because there are no seasonal changes in climate to upset life patterns. Consequently, more varieties of highly specialized life-styles have been able to evolve and persist. But biological specialists tend to be high-risk types. If a biological generalist such as the orang-utan, which feeds on a large number of different kinds of plants, runs out of its favorite food, it has many other choices and won't starve to death. But what of the specialist that eats only one kind of plant? If disease wipes out that plant, the specialist also is wiped out, unless it happens to have genes that enable it to turn to another food plant as a substitute.

Biological specialists are much more sensitive to environmental change than the generalists are. Temperature, humidity, nutrient availability, and adequate space are only a few of the environmental conditions to which the specialists and generalists alike are finely tuned. Only a small change in one or more of those environmental factors could spell doom for a species. The great number and wide variety of

Dominican botanist Alexander, chief scientist at the island's scientific research center, explains to the author the importance of multiple crop experimentation. The island's farmers, he says, must move away from bananas as their main crop. They must learn to "intercrop" with citrus fruits, melons, tropical flowers, and other cash crops to round out their productivity.

highly specialized plant-animal relationships is one of the major reasons a tropical rain forest is such a fragile place, one so easily upset or destroyed. At the same time, those vast numbers of differences in species, in living habits, and in associations are the very strength of the forest.

In a word, diversity is a tropical rain forest's avenue to success. And in the long run it may be the key to the success of the species known as *Homo sapiens*. If that is so, what are the values of a tropical rain forest?

6

VALUES
OF THE
RAIN FORESTS

When Columbus visited the West Indies in the late 1400s he described the islands' tropical forests in his report to Spain's Ferdinand and Isabella:

> *Its lands are high; there are in it many sierras and very lofty mountains. . . . All are most beautiful, of a thousand shapes; all are accessible and are filled with trees of a thousand kinds and tall, so that they seem to touch the sky. I am told that they never lose their foliage, and this I can believe, for I saw them as green and lovely as they are in Spain in May, and some of them were flowering, some bearing fruit, and some at another stage, according to their nature.*

Tropical rain forests of the equatorial region differ from other forests in two important ways—a large amount of rain (160 to 400 inches, or 406 to 1,016 centimeters, per year) and a high yearly average temperature (78°F, or 25.5°C), without a dry season or marked cold. These conditions give the forests the unchanging color and lushness observed by Columbus.

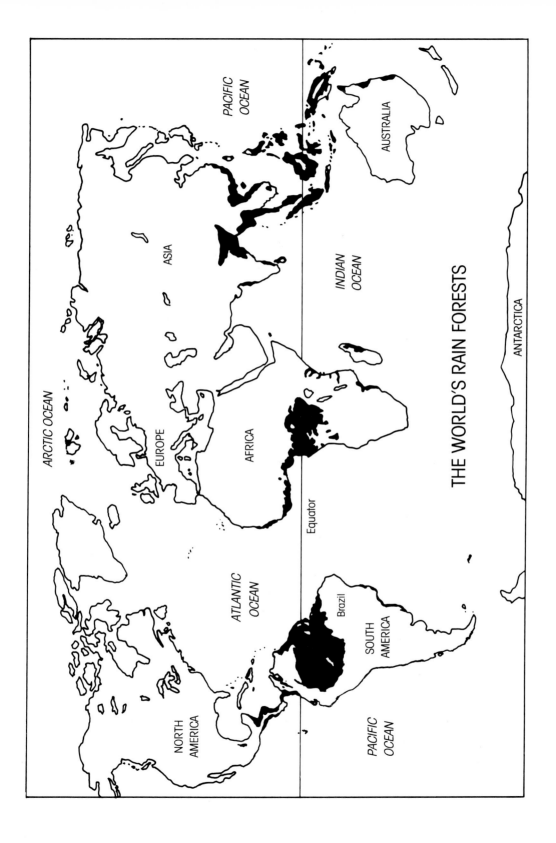

THE WORLD'S RAIN FORESTS

Types of Tropical Forests

Tropical rain forests trace a green belt around the planet from 30°N to 20°S of the equator. Although parts of the tropical forest global region, or biome, are drenched in rain all year long, others farther north and south have one or two relatively dry periods. These forests are called tropical moist forests, or tropical deciduous forests. Two-thirds of all rain forests are the wet equatorial type. One that is unique, and that we will visit in Chapter 8, is a temperate rain forest in the state of Washington, the Hoh Rain Forest.

The world's largest wet rain forest regions are South America's Amazon Basin, the East Indies (Sumatra, Borneo, and Papua New Guinea), and Africa's Congo Basin. But many islands of the south Pacific Ocean are also part of this forest biome. Tropical deciduous forests are also scattered around the equatorial belt. India, Southeast Asia, and southern Africa have large regions of them. Smaller deciduous forest regions are found in Yucatán, the Caribbean islands, and southern Florida.

The global air circulation patterns are what keep the equatorial tropical forests wet. By day, energy from the sun heats the land. The moist air above the ground is heated and rises high into the atmosphere. As the air rises it is cooled, and its moisture falls out as rain. Meanwhile, more moist air is drawn in from the oceans to replace the rising air. In this way there is an endless supply of moist air rising above the equator and an endless supply of rain.

What good is a rain forest? Why should we care that they are vanishing faster than any other ecosystem? That nearly one-fifth of all the tropical rain forests now standing will be gone or plundered by the year 2000?

Tropical rain forests serve us, and their inhabitants, in many ways: They supply wood for fuel and construction materials. They keep the soil intact and prevent erosion during heavy rains. They are important agents of climate control, a source of many foods and medicines, and

Tropical and semitropical regions have tropical deciduous forests in addition to their rain forests. The lush growth of the tropical deciduous forest shown here is characteristic of certain parts of central and southern Florida. This photograph was taken on a river near New Port Richey. The water was so still it is hard to find the shore line.

a home for numerous people and other animal species. The forests produce bananas, coffee, eggplants, lemons, limes, oranges, tea, cacao, cashews, cassava, peanuts, pineapples, papayas, guavas, mangos, and many other edible plants. As the forests are logged and cleared for farming or for pastureland, their soils erode and the diversity of their plant and animal life suffers greatly.

Medicinal Plants

English explorer Charles Waterton was one of the first to test a tropical rain forest plant's value as medicine. Traveling through Guyana in 1814, he witnessed the preparation of a substance the natives used to coat the tips of their arrows in order to kill game quickly by poisoning. Curious about how the poison worked, he brought a sample back to London and injected a dose into a donkey. Within ten minutes the donkey stopped breathing, collapsed, and appeared dead. Waterton applied artificial respiration for two hours by pumping air through an opening he made in the donkey's windpipe. Within another two hours the donkey stood up and began walking around as if nothing had happened.

The mysterious substance was curare, the juice of a South American liana, or climbing plant. Used in strong concentrations, curare completely relaxes muscles, including the diaphragm and heart. As one Indian medicine man told European explorer Alexander von Humboldt in 1800, "Curare which we prepare is far superior to [your gun powder]. It is the juice of a plant which kills quietly without one knowing whence the blow came." In 1541 a party of explorers led by the Spaniard Francisco de Orellana was dumbfounded when one of its members was struck in the finger by an arrow and died within a few minutes.

There are three different types of curare, each from a different liana. Curare is extremely useful as a medicine when used in small doses and when the patient is kept breathing. For example, it is an ideal muscle relaxant for delicate operations involving the eye and abdomen. If you ever get stuck with an arrow that has been dipped in curare, take a dose of physostigmine, a drug that counteracts the effects of curare. Physostigmine comes from a West African bean plant. The drug also is useful for treating glaucoma, an eye disease.

Brazilian Indians of the Urueu-Wau-Wau tribe tip their arrows and spears with a poisonous sap squeezed from the red bark of the *tiki uba* tree. The sap prevents clotting of blood, causing victims to bleed to death. It may turn out to be an important pharmaceutical find.

The poisonous substances (a class of chemicals called alkaloids) developed by plants serve the plants as a defense against insect enemies, at least until the insects evolve their own chemical defense against the alkaloids. Cancer researchers at Bethesda, Maryland's National Cancer Institute are especially interested in alkaloids of the tropical rain forests as a promising source of drugs for the treatment of cancer. The institute has identified more than 2,000 tropical plants with anti-cancer properties. About sixty alkaloids have been identified in a single periwinkle plant found on the island of Madagascar off Africa's southeast coast. Some are used to treat tumors, leukemia, and Hodgkin's disease. Fifteen tons of periwinkle leaves are needed to make one ounce of vincristine, an anti-cancer agent. The 1985 price of vincristine was $100,000 a pound!

Botanists believe that there are many more tropical "miracle plants" awaiting discovery. Scientists who studied 1,500 plants from Costa Rica's rain forests say that 225 may be helpful in treating cancer. Clues about the healing powers of various plants sometimes come from medicine men or medicine women of tropical forest tribes, and knowledge of such plants often goes back several thousand years. South America's ipecac plant is one such old-timer among medicinal plants. It is the most effective agent for the treatment of the very unpleasant intestinal disease amoebic dysentery. Another old-timer is a shrub that has been used as a tranquilizer in India for thousands of years. Kina, the classic drug used against malaria, comes from the bark of the cinchona plant in the western Amazon, and aspirin originated with willow bark. Roughly 25 percent of all the prescription drugs we buy in our drugstores come from plants. In all, about 7,000 medicines used by modern physicians come from tropical forest plants.

As destruction of the rain forests continues, botanists, medical scientists, and others fear that untold numbers of lifesaving medicinal and other useful plants not yet identified may be destroyed. We are just now beginning to learn some of the seemingly endless ways that products of tropical rain forests can be used. But if the present rate of forest destruction continues, there will be only scattered patches of accessible tropical forests left after the turn of the century. To date, we have studied only 1 percent of tropical rain forest species for their broad spectrum of usefulness.

Rain Forests as Gene Pools

Genes are those biological units of inheritance that determine whether you are tall or short, whether your eyes are brown or blue, and, if you happen to be a plant, whether you have wrinkled or smooth bark or whether or not you shed your leaves in the fall.

The population of New York City is made up of people from many parts of the world—there are Hispanics, Chinese, African Americans, Haitians, Japanese, and many others. In the population as a whole there are genes for black skin, tan skin, white skin, tallness, shortness, and all the other characteristics of all the different racial and cultural types of people. In other words, New York City's total population has a very large assortment of different kinds of genes, or a highly varied gene pool. By comparison, the Chinese of the city's Chinatown or the African Americans of Harlem have fewer different kinds of genes; that is, the gene pools of those two subpopulations are not so highly varied.

We can speak of the gene pools of different populations of organisms living in a small pond or of the gene pools of a tropical forest.

No one knows how many different kinds, or species, of plants and animals exist. The total number of tropical and subtropical species alone may be as high as thirty million, according to a 1989 report to the U.S. National Science Board. A typical small lake in the Amazon contains about 100 fish species compared with only a half dozen or so fish species in a typical Maine lake.

The tropical rain forests harbor the largest gene pools on the planet. These gene pools are the most important biological resource available to us, life's memory bank that has evolved and grown over thousands of millions of years. Brazil's Amazon Basin has a million animal and plant species, including 1,800 bird species and 2,000 fish species. Of all the tropical rain forest areas, Amazonia is the largest single genetic reservoir. Collectively, these forests are nature's main library of information about an infinite variety of biological achievements.

When a small section of wet tropical forest is cleared and then allowed to regrow naturally, the area of new growth is called a secondary forest. Gradually the secondary forest regains much of the former species diversity as plants and animals from the surrounding primary forest invade it.

But the picture changes when a large area of primary forest by the forest's edge is cleared by loggers and damaged by their destructive machines. If left to heal itself naturally, the area is not likely to regain its former species diversity and will tend to be left with a permanently weakened species structure and a diluted gene pool. Soils that pave a tropical rain forest's floor tend to be shallow and to store relatively few nutrients. When the trees are cut down and hauled away, the fragile soil structure is destroyed by the wheels and metal tracks of logging machines. Now exposed to sunlight and the impact of heavy rain, the soil is further damaged by drying and erosion. Key plant species and the animals that depend on them may be lost to the area for many centuries, or forever. In such cases, destruction is irreversible, as is the loss of genetic diversity due to a decline in the forest's gene pool.

Why Is Genetic Diversity Important?

Today farmers in many regions of the world depend on large yields of a single crop, such as corn or wheat. Such monocultures, or single-crop cultures, tend to rely heavily on fertilizers as a source of nutrients and on pesticides to keep the bugs away. Even so, insect pests or disease claim a crop or an entire species from time to time. For example, in the 1970s the citrus fruit known as jeruk Bali was wiped out in Indonesia by a killer virus. Such calamaties tend to occur when a plant has been continuously bred by man, because the plant's genetic variety is weakened. A solution to the problem of gene-poor food plants is to crossbreed them with wild-type plants and thereby enhance their natural defenses through gene enrichment. Farmers in many parts of the world have long known that they can fight pests and plant diseases and overcome the limitations of poor soils and unfavorable weather conditions by breeding several different genetic varieties of a crop. Farmers on Papua New Guinea, for instance, grow 200 types of taro, their major crop. Each variety has a different assortment of genes. Some varieties have a natural resistance to drought, and others have a built-in resistance to certain insect pests or plant diseases. This genetic variety provides the best possible protection against a massive crop failure due to a single cause.

The long-term health of modern varieties of food plants grown on a large scale depends on the genes of wild plants from the world's forests. But as the rapid destruction of tropical rain forests continues, the much needed wild species so important to modern agriculture are fast disappearing, along with their marvelously rich gene pools.

The value of tropical rain forests reaches beyond the edges of their gene pools. Their values seem to extend high into the atmosphere where the forces of weather and climate are fashioned.

7

RAIN FORESTS AND CLIMATE CHANGE

The clatter set up by a torrential downpour in a tropical rain forest has to be experienced to be appreciated. The noise comes not from rain splashing on the ground but from the heights above in the canopy. If the canopy is healthy and dense, the light dims and the air grows so heavy that you can almost chew it. The battering force of the raindrops is borne by the network of leaves high overhead. Water reaches the ground in infinite tiny streams trickling along the tangle of vines and down the broad tree trunks. Instead of assaulting the ground, the rainwater is silently, quickly, and efficiently absorbed by the spongelike mat that is the forest floor. An inch of rain commonly falls in half an hour, forty times the rainfall of an average New Hampshire summer shower. In some tropical rain forests eight inches of rain may cascade onto the canopy in only one hour.

How Rain Forests Conserve Water

Even where a section of rain forest blankets a steep hillside, the ground is not eroded. Instead, the trees and shrubby growth serve the surrounding land well by acting as a vast living reservoir that absorbs the water quickly but releases it slowly and in moderation. Nearby

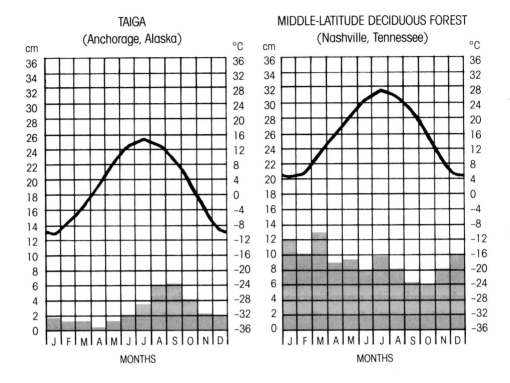

TAIGA
(Anchorage, Alaska)

MIDDLE-LATITUDE DECIDUOUS FOREST
(Nashville, Tennessee)

MONTHS

MONTHS

rivers and farmland that are farther down the hill are not suddenly and destructively flooded but are cushioned by the moderating authority of the forest. If the forest is shaved off the slope, the land is exposed to the full destructive force of the water from tropical storms. The result—rapid erosion and landslides.

So the forest plays two important roles: If left alone, it protects and preserves itself, and by so doing it assures that a just supply of water is available to all throughout the year, preventing both drought and flooding. Only when the forest is destroyed do drought and flooding ravage the land. The World Wildlife Fund reports that 40 percent of farmers living in villages associated with a tropical rain forest region rely on the forest to protect them from drought and flood. If the forest is damaged, the village either washes away or dries up.

Between 1960 and 1980 India cut more than 16,000 square miles of its forests, an area twice the size of Massachusetts. Today less than 15 percent of India's land remains covered with forest growth. As a

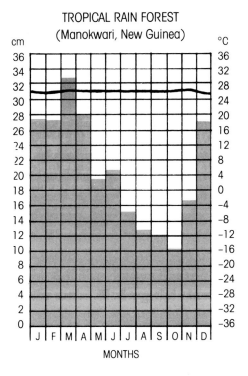

TROPICAL RAIN FOREST
(Manokwari, New Guinea)

cm — °C

MONTHS

High temperatures and abundant rain throughout the year combine to make tropical rain forests rich, varied, and fast growing. Compare these three "climatograms" for monthly rainfall (shown in the bar columns) and monthly temperature change (heavy solid line across each bar graph). Rainfall is shown in centimeters at the left of each graph. Temperature is shown in degrees Celsius at the right of each graph.

result of forest loss, drought is now common and predictable. Long-dependable mountain springs are drying up, and dust from the drying soil pollutes the air. According to Mohan Dharia, an environmentalist, "At the rate we are destroying our forests we will not have to wait for long to see India become the biggest desert in the world."

Much of the rain that falls into a tropical forest during a heavy storm is caught by the leaves and vines of the canopy and retained until it evaporates. Rain trickling down to the forest floor seeps into the soil where some is taken up by roots, some feeds springs, and the rest finds its way through the sponge matrix into streams and rivers. During a brief and gentle shower, almost all of the rain is kept by the canopy. During my travels through the rain forest of Dominica, I was constantly amazed by the clearness and purity of the streams and small rivers, all of which were drinkable and refreshingly cool whenever I had to wade across them.

When a forest is cleared, rainwater falling on the cleared area is

When forest is cleared on a slope, the land no longer acts as a sponge that controls the water from heavy rains. Instead, the slopes are gullied and the soil washed into streams and rivers. Clear-cutting contributes both to flooding and drought.

no longer managed. Instead of being efficiently absorbed, the torrents of water that batter the exposed ground quickly run off and wash away humus and other soil components. By the time a downpour stops, rivers originating in the cut forest region quickly swell with the runoff of cloudy water laden with silt. The rapid rise is then felt downstream, where local flooding may occur. After the rainy season, the cut forest area has no water budget left and the rivers run dry until the next heavy rain. Villages downstream may be stricken by drought. The periodic destructive floods along the Ganges plains and east central Bangladesh are caused by the deforestation of the slopes of the Himalayan mountains. Runoff from the Himalayan slopes dumps so much soil into the Ganges that every square mile of that river's water contains about 4,000 tons of soil. Compare that with the muddy Mississippi River's 250 tons per square mile of water.

The steeper a slope left bare after a tropical rain forest has been cut, the greater the soil loss by erosion. In all such cases the runoff burdened with eroded soil ends up in a stream and then a river. Along Africa's Ivory Coast, for example, one acre of deforested shallow slope may lose 6,000 times more soil due to runoff than an area that has not been deforested. The sediments in the runoff are carried downstream and deposited at the mouth of the river, where they build a network of soft islands and mud bars called a delta. The delta at the mouth of the Mississippi, for instance, has been building for more than 500,000 years. As a result, its sediments of washed-away topsoil are more than 3.8 miles deep. Sediments carried seaward by the Ganges are thought to be about 9.5 miles thick. When a dam happens to interrupt the flow of a river, the water-borne sediments are trapped and accumulate behind the dam. Eventually the sediments choke the dam into a state of uselessness. Many dams in the tropics have met that fate, largely as a result of deforestation. The dams are filling up with sediments four to six times faster than was expected when the dams were built. Sometimes we learn by our mistakes; other times we do not learn, and we keep repeating them.

How Rain Forests Affect Local Climate

When water evaporates, the liquid water changes into a dry gas called water vapor. A lot of water vapor in the air makes the weather "muggy." If there is little water vapor, the air is dry. The amount of water that a tropical rain forest's early morning veil of mist returns to the air through evaporation is enormous. In forests such as those making up the Amazon, well over 50 percent of the rainfall consists of water previously transpired and evaporated from the forest. A grassland returns only 40 percent, and bare soil only 30 percent. As a result of the highly efficient water budget of tropical rain forests, precipitation in the tropical belt may be more than three times the world average of 30 inches. Among the wettest tropical rain forests is Colombia's Choco forest, where an average of 400 inches of rain falls each year. That's 33 feet! The abundant rain is caused by moist air that flows landward from the Pacific Ocean and is then forced up the slopes of the Andes. Cooled aloft, the air releases its plentiful moisture as rain.

The broader and higher a forest, the larger its water budget and the more water the forest returns to atmospheric circulation. This is still another moderating influence of the forest—controlling local climate by preventing alternating periods of excessive dryness and excessive wetness. The amount of humidity and the temperature are prevented from taking large leaps up and down. Both of these elements of climate are important to successful agriculture. After one part of Central America cleared its tropical rain forests, average rainfall in the area dropped by 17 inches. The Sahelian droughts in Africa that seem to be expanding the Sahara could be related to the destruction of rain forests in West and Central Africa.

The unevenness of the top of the forest canopy is another important characteristic that influences local climate. Air flowing over the forest top is slowed and roughened into turbulent motion, which can be upsetting to a passenger in a low-flying small plane. The turbulence causes large parcels of moisture-laden air to rise into cooler regions of the atmosphere. There the water vapor condenses as clouds, which then release rain. Over those regions of the Amazon where the forest has not been disturbed, great pillars of towering cumulus clouds are a common sight. But such rain clouds are noticeably absent over regions that have been cut and where the ground is parched. On Dominica nearly every mountain peak is reassuringly concealed within a little cloud.

Do Rain Forests Affect Global Climate?

The past few years have seen a growing concern over the likelihood that human activity influences climate change on a global scale. It is clear that deforestation of the world's tropical rain forest reserves does change local climates by tampering with the water budget. It is less certain that deforestation is contributing to global climate change, although signs point in that direction.

Whenever we burn fossil fuels (wood, coal, fuel oil, or natural gas), carbon dioxide and other substances are released into the air. The by-products of burning fossil fuels are called "greenhouse" gases, and carbon dioxide is the major one. Other greenhouse gases—methane, water vapor, and nitrous oxides, for example—play a lesser role. The greenhouse gases hang in the air and form a one-way heat filter. While they allow short-wave radiation from the Sun to pass through to the ground, they trap the long-wave heat radiation given off by Earth's surface. The glass of a greenhouse traps heat in the same way, hence the term "greenhouse effect."

Virtually all scientists who have studied the greenhouse effect agree that a slow but measurable warming (between 0.3°C and 0.6°C) of the atmosphere has been taking place over the past century. Some say that the warming is a result of human activity that has added large amounts of carbon dioxide and other greenhouse gases to the air. They further contend that serious warming almost certainly is on the way, but that it may be several more years before they can predict this effect with a "high degree of confidence." The warming will probably be

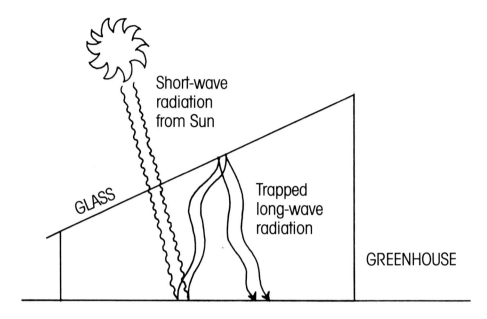

Short-wave radiation from the Sun striking Earth's surface is absorbed and re-emitted as long-wave (heat) radiation. In a greenhouse, the long-wave radiation is trapped because it cannot pass through the glass, although short-wave radiation can. Outside, cloud cover and greenhouse gases such as carbon dioxide act as a greenhouse's glass, trapping the long-wave radiation.

large enough to have socially significant effects, according to a major report of the International Panel on Climate Change (IPCC).

According to the Worldwatch Institute, atmospheric carbon dioxide has increased 24 percent since 1860, and about half of that increase has occurred since 1958. Today we are adding to the atmosphere's carbon dioxide reservoir at the rate of 4 percent a year. If that rate continues, the planet could heat up by 1.5°C to 4.5°C by the year 2030, say the IPCC scientists. As the warming continues, scientists predict that the polar ice caps will begin to melt, causing a slow rise in sea level that will flood many of the world's coastal cities. Some experts expect that sea level will rise by as much as four feet by the year 2050. Others think the rise may be closer to only one foot.

It would seem prudent to slow the rate at which we are adding to the atmosphere's carbon dioxide reservoir. If we could slow it to 2 percent a year, the big heat might not arrive until the year 2050. That twenty-year delay could give us time to breed new crops capable of tolerating heat and drought, to redesign and rebuild selected port cities, and to relocate endangered coastal populations inland. Unfortunately, the reality of such a cutback in carbon dioxide addition to the air seems remote—the present rate is expected to *double* over the next forty years as the world population continues to grow and as Third World nations develop new industries.

At the present rate of growth, by the middle of the next century there will not be five billion people living on this planet—there will be ten billion!

The ever increasing burning of fossil fuels by factories and the mushrooming world population are at the root of the warming trend. Until the machines of industrial nations began overloading the atmosphere with carbon dioxide, about half remained in the atmosphere and the remaining 50 percent was absorbed by the oceans and forests, especially the tropical forests. The forests gobble up carbon dioxide during photosynthesis. According to George M. Woodwell, director of the Ecosystems Center at the Marine Biological Laboratory in Woods Hole, Massachusetts, "the emphasis is on the forests because they are extensive in area, conduct more photosynthesis worldwide than any other type of vegetation, and have the potential for storing carbon in quantities that are sufficiently large to affect the carbon dioxide content of the atmosphere." In Woodwell's view, "it is difficult to avoid the conclusion that the destruction of the forests of the world is adding carbon dioxide to the atmosphere at a rate comparable to the rate of release for the combustion of fossil fuels."

The bulk of carbon dioxide released into the air by forest destruction comes from the tropics. According to the Worldwatch Institute: "40 percent of the total net release of carbon from tropical forest land conversion comes from tropical America, 37 percent from tropical Asia, and 23 percent from tropical Africa. Just five countries account for half of all net carbon releases from deforestation; the loss of forests in Brazil alone contributes one-fifth of the total."

Two Scenarios for the Future

At this stage in our meager knowledge about the relationships between forest destruction and global climate change, even the experts admit that they are making "educated guesses." All agree that the cutting and burning of forests is adding a significant amount of carbon dioxide to the air. But what happens to all that carbon dioxide? The experts do not agree, and the ultimate scenario that most of them can accept has yet to be written. Two conflicting views reflect the disagreement.

Both agree that carbon dioxide released by the cutting and burning of tropical forests is heating the planet. No one denies this, but what the long-term result will be is unknown.

One view is that increased carbon dioxide levels might increase the growth rate of the remaining forests, because carbon dioxide (along with water) is an essential "food" for the growth of green plants. The increased growth rate would remove more carbon dioxide from the atmosphere, which would ease the greenhouse warming. But to date there is no convincing evidence that braking action on global heating would actually take place.

Another scenario, the one favored by Woodwell, predicts that the buildup of atmospheric carbon dioxide might increase the rate of respiration of trees. By day, in the presence of sunlight, trees take in carbon dioxide as they carry on photosynthesis. By night and day, they carry out respiration, during which they give off carbon dioxide. Trees that have shed their leaves in the fall are unable to carry on photosynthesis until they grow new leaves in the spring, so in winter they produce more carbon dioxide than they take in. A vicious cycle is set in motion: Increased warming speeds respiration. Increased respiration adds increased amounts of atmospheric carbon dioxide. Increased atmospheric carbon dioxide speeds the warming. And so on.

When respiration is more rapid than photosynthesis over a long time, trees stop growing and die. As forests die, the decay of their remains continues to feed large amounts of carbon dioxide into the air. As Woodwell points out, "the sudden destruction of forests by air pollution, now being experienced in northern and central Europe and in the eastern mountains of North America, is but a sample of the destruction that appears to be in store."

Climate Is a Complex Affair

Lack of agreement about how the world's forests eventually will respond to global warming is cause for deep concern. But of even deeper concern is the experts' consensus that global warming has already begun in response to the buildup of atmospheric carbon dioxide.

Climate is a complex affair and it depends on so many things—energy cycles of the Sun, global shifts in wind and ocean current patterns, and the health of the ozone layer, to name a few. No one can say with certainty what Earth's climate will be fifty or a hundred years from now. However, climatologists look for trends, such as the known buildup of greenhouse gases in the atmosphere. The 1980s had the hottest four years of any decade since 1900. On the basis of a warming trend that seems to be speeding up, NASA's climatologist James Hansen has said that he is "99 percent" certain that the greenhouse effect has started. "It has been detected and is changing our climate now," he told a U.S. Senate committee hearing in June 1988. In 1989 Hansen told Congress that his computer climate modeling causes him to expect "drought intensification at most middle- and low-altitude land areas." Many of Hansen's colleagues do not share his trust in computer climate models and think that his long-range weather outlook is questionable. Hansen and his supporters do not agree.

Effects of a long-term warming would differ in different parts of the world, according to climatologists. Shifting wind patterns might increase rainfall over parts of Africa that are presently relatively dry, for example. Growing seasons might be lengthened in part of the Soviet Union, Canada, and Scandinavia. The United States might be less lucky and watch its wheat and corn belts dry up with 40 percent less rainfall than now. Water tables in such regions would drop, and in regions along the coast, water supplies would become useless as they became invaded by salt water. Lake Michigan would begin to evaporate, causing vast areas of reeking mud to surface around Chicago.

Is there a workable solution to the global warming problem, which, in part at least, seems linked to the collective health of the world's tropical forests? If so, neither the economists nor the politicians have produced one. The future of tropical forests may well be determined by how well tropical forest ecologists are able to educate the public about the many ways in which the forests sustain and enrich our lives, not only materially, but spiritually as well.

Because the forests' effects on global climate are not restricted to tropical rain forests, we will now broaden our view to include primary forest destruction in the United States. Like Brazil's tropical rain forest, the monarch forests of the Pacific Northwest are fast disappearing.

8
TOO LATE FOR THE PACIFIC NORTHWEST?

When I returned from the unspoiled tropical rain forest of Dominica, I dried out my backpack and restocked it with things I would need for hiking through Washington's Olympic Rain Forest and then eastward into the Cascade range to see firsthand how our forests at home are faring.

I had been reading about the controversy, bitter and sometimes violent, over the widespread cutting of the old-growth forests in northern California, Oregon, Washington, and Alaska. But I was not prepared for the devastation of primary forest that I saw for mile after endless mile during my drive through parts of the state of Washington.

On first seeing the east coast of North America in 1524, Spanish explorer Verrazano described it as "a land full of the largest forests . . . with as much beauty and delectable appearance as it would be possible to express." He would have been even more impressed by the forests of the Pacific Northwest. With their Douglas fir and Sitka spruce, they were until recently the greatest coniferous forests on earth.

The Pacific Northwest forest stretches from Alaska southward for about 2,000 miles to San Francisco. It ranges another seventy-five or so miles inland to the Cascade range. Many of its majestic trees are 500 years old, and some have reached an age of 2,000 years. All are targets for the snarling chain saws of the timber industry and the Forest Service.

"A Shocking Desecration"

Mile after mile of the steep mountain slopes are bare of trees. In their place are broad stumps, often blackened by the loggers' match, and the ground is littered with severed tree limbs. The soil, exposed to the weather, is cut by trenches eroded by rain. Countless miles of logging roads bulldozed by the timber industry and the U.S. Forest Service gleam in the sunlight as a network of endlessly winding ribbons. The hills are as empty and spooky to view as the deserts of Syria and Lebanon, themselves once covered with vast cedar forests from which Solomon cut trees to build the temple at Jerusalem.

Farther south is another special region of forest. It is a narrow strip some 20 miles wide by 450 miles long. There is no other area like it on Earth. In its scattered groves on the western slopes of the California Sierras stand the great redwood trees. Some of these giants are more than 300 feet high, weigh more than 1,000 tons, and are 1,000 or more years old. Among the redwoods are huge sugar pines and incense cedar with their sweet odor.

It takes a thousand years or more for nature to grow a redwood, but it takes only minutes to cut one down. Two hundred years ago California had an estimated two million acres of redwood forests, but only about 85,000 virgin acres remain. About 150 old-growth redwoods are toppled each day. Conservation groups such as the Sierra Club are trying to stop the destruction of the redwood trees, but lumber companies such as Louisiana-Pacific and Pacific Lumber fight back and continue to cut the trees. Once the redwood trees are gone, they will disappear from the planet forever. Nothing can bring them back because evolution does not repeat itself.

The Forest Service tries to hide the ugliness of its work from the public in Washington by leaving a narrow strip of tall trees between the highway and the clear-cut area. "Visual protection corridors" is the term it uses to describe the thin and deceitful tree borders. However, no one can hide a sprawling area of shaved-off mountainside. It is like the proverbial ostrich trying to hide by burying its head in the sand.

Realizing that the public cannot be so easily fooled, Washington's Department of Natural Resources just cuts everything right up to the roadside. According to one of its brochures: "Our practice of not leaving a narrow strip of trees along the highway may be questioned. But we do that to ensure motorist safety. Conifers left standing in narrow, open rows are more likely to be blown over by winds."

Wyoming's Senator Gale McGee calls clear-cutting "a shocking desecration that has to be seen to be believed." A stroll across a crater of the Moon would be more inviting than setting foot in a clear-cut area.

The Hoh Rain Forest

"Hey, Dad, look at this one!" my son called out as Deb, his wife, and I caught up with him. His nose was six inches away from the cut surface of a Douglas fir as he walked his fingers across the broad field of annual growth rings. Dry periods had slowed the tree's growth for five years when the tree was 147 years old. There were good years and poor years for the five-foot diameter tree. Years earlier it had been toppled by a storm. Forest park rangers had then cut out a section so that hikers like us could walk through and stay on the trail. By the time Jim had reached ring number 223, he was in another dry period. The rings were so close together that he gave up counting. We guessed the tree was at least 250 years old.

We were in the Hoh Rain Forest of Olympic National Park about ten miles northwest of snow-capped Mount Olympus. We had hiked the Hall of Mosses trail and were now a mile or so along the Hoh River trail. Roosevelt elk, found only in this area, are common, signs of them

Son James lost count of the annual growth rings of this Douglas fir tree of the Olympic Peninsula, but he estimated its age as close to 250 years. Trees in regions that have growing seasons alternating with seasons of dormancy have growth rings. But in a tropical rain forest the growing season is continuous, so trees there lack annual growth rings. How do we count their age? We don't.

being everywhere. Preservation of the elk was one reason why the region was declared a national park. The elk keep the forest floor from becoming a dense jungle of salmonberry and vine maple. Nevertheless, every inch of the forest floor is carpeted with plant growth and is soft and spongy underfoot.

The forest is a symphony of a thousand tints of green. Sword ferns and more than one hundred species of mosses and lichens seem to cover everything—rocks, rotting stumps, and the limbs that litter the forest floor. Moss hangs in endless draperies from the tree branches high above. Vine maple leaves and low tree branches filter the light through arching, moss-draped bowers. The air of the dimly lit forest is eternally moist, still, and heavily scented with the sweet odor of decay. Wind in the upper story of the forest barely reaches the floor. Where the ground is wet, sorrel and water parsley are abundant. So are slugs about five inches long. There are striped slugs, spotted slugs, green

Daughter-in-law Deb and the author stretch across a moss-covered monarch in the Hoh Rain Forest on Washington's Olympic Peninsula. Many of these centuries-old Douglas fir trees are six feet or more in diameter. Loggers will not get these since they are on national park land.

slugs, brown slugs, and, unavoidably, squashed slugs. Their numbers and styles of dress are endless. A common sound is the scolding *chip, chip, chip* of a Douglas squirrel, a warning that you are in its territory. This squirrel species is found only in this region. Ruffed grouse and bald eagles also make this forest their home (and eat the squirrels for dinner).

The high canopy of spruce, cedar, and hemlock acts as an umbrella that protects the forest floor from the beating rains. But much of the twelve feet of precipitation that bathes the forest each year comes as a misty veil that hangs throughout the forest day and night. The rains here seldom fall in torrents.

Many of the big trees stretch more than 200 feet skyward. Unlike a tropical rain forest, this is a temperate coniferous rain forest whose fir and spruce trees have needles sharp to the touch. When a big tree falls, it provides a stage for new life. Hemlock and spruce seedlings, unable to survive on the tangled forest floor, take up life on the fallen and rotting tree trunks. They absorb minerals, moisture, and warmth from the decaying trunks. But even on this perch competition is fierce. The seedlings that survive put out roots that reach down and grow into the soil. Eventually their "nurse log" decays, leaving a soldierlike row of young trees neatly columned and poised above the ground on rooted stilts.

A 500-year-old Douglas fir that is toppled by weather or age lives on in other ways as well, perhaps for another 500 years. Its rough bark provides nesting space for folding-door spiders; moss, shelf fungi, and other decomposers sprout from the fallen tree and begin their long assignment of decomposition. Beetles, ants, armies of termites, and other insects invade the fallen tree. Voles, pseudoscorpions, centipedes, and creatures with such unfamiliar names as oribatids and earwigs pry apart the rotting bark in search of a meal or shelter. Martens, spotted owls, and other larger predators often breakfast on or around the fallen tree. Stands of old-growth trees provide a habitat for more than forty species. Although tropical rain forests display a greater diversity of life than a temperate rain forest does, acre for acre a temperate rain forest has seven times more living matter.

Clear-Cutting the Pacific Northwest

Leaving the Olympic National Park is like leaving a botanical garden and entering a war zone. Just outside the park, the land has been ravaged by the loggers' artillery—snarling chain saws, skidders, and bulldozers. Most of the landscape, once primary forest, has been clearcut. The charred remains of burned stumps of old-growth trees stick up through the rutted soil of the former forest floor as black tombstones. Only occasionally are there patches of green forest. The view is the same all along the twenty-five miles of national park road and then along Route 101 into the logging town of Forks, Washington.

It is in Forks that much of the drama of forest destruction in Washington is written. This is where deals are made to sell off the old-growth forests of the state. Practically every restaurant and shop hangs a handwritten notice in its window telling patrons that "Logging dollars support this establishment." Many of the modest houses of loggers and their families display hand-painted signs reading, "This family is supported by timber dollars." One dirt side road just outside Forks had a sign reading, "26 logging families live on this road and are supported by logging dollars." One sign in Forks reads, "Support the timber industry. If you are not part of the solution, you are part of the problem."

A brochure sponsored by the Washington Department of Natural Resources tells readers that "it is not readily apparent to U.S. Highway 101 travelers that the logged areas all along the route are giving birth to a new generation of forests. Although the recently logged areas will be unattractive for a time, new trees are growing rapidly. Modern forest management practices, including clear-cutting, shorten the time it takes to regenerate the forest and increase the volume of wood for future harvests. . . . Enjoy the sights and sounds of our growing forests."

What the state's Department of Natural Resources doesn't tell the readers of its brochure is that clear-cutting a primary forest destroys forever not only the forest, but its vital diversity. The loggers move in and cut everything in sight—the softwood pines and firs and the hardwood oaks and cedars. Then the Forest Service replants with only a few species valued by the timber industry. "They're converting complex, old-growth ecosystems . . . into monocultures," according to Jeff DeBonis, founder of the Association of Forest Service Employees for Environmental Ethics.

A "managed" forest grown and regrown on clear-cut land is not a natural forest. For as long as it is "managed" it will never be given time to regenerate its original biodiversity, or the old-growth trees that the loggers most prize and cut as fast as they can, out of fear that they will be made to stop. Each day 170 acres of the old-growth trees fall to the chain saw. According to Peter Morrison of Seattle's Wilderness Society, three-quarters of the old-growth trees have already been cut in the Olympic National Forest, which is public land. At the present rate of cutting, the rest will be gone in 14 years. "It's one of the worst environmental disasters ever to beset the Northwest," he said.

Driving along Route 101, within a space of fifteen minutes I counted twenty-seven logging trucks, each carrying only old-growth trees of giant Sitka spruce and Douglas fir centuries old. Now nearly gone, they once stood as part of the monarch forests of the world. Ecologists refer to the ancient giants as "old-growth" trees; the loggers scornfully term them "overage" and "decadent." Already, 90 percent of the monarch forests of the U.S. Pacific Northwest have been cut and hauled to the mill to be ground up as toothpicks or made into disposable diapers. Canada has chopped down 60 percent of its share. Less than 5 percent survives on the entire North American continent, and most of that is on public land.

The state's Department of Natural Resources does not admit that genetic diversity is lost when a primary forest is destroyed and replaced by a forest managed by the timber industry. Nor does it mention the

Top: When nature destroys a forest, as during the Mount St. Helens eruption, most plant species recover and restore the diversity of the old forest. Bottom: When man clear cuts a primary forest, the replacement secondary forest lacks the original diversity since the timber industry replants and favors only the kinds of trees it finds commercially valuable. Diversity is an important measure of a forest's health.

illegal destruction of vital watersheds when certain forest areas are recklessly clear-cut. It does not acknowledge the habitat destruction that forces wildlife to move elsewhere, or more often perish.

Role of the U.S. Forest Service

Can the U.S. Forest Service help? In 1897, Congress decided that the nation's forests should be managed to protect watersheds and "to furnish a continuous supply of timber for the use and necessities of citizens of the United States." But the Forest Service also was charged with the preservation of wilderness. Until a few decades ago, the timber industry pressured the Forest Service to keep the timber of the national forests off the commercial market in order to prevent the government from competing with the privately owned timber holdings. The Forest Service did just that—until the 1960s when the timber companies realized that they had cut nearly everything in sight on their privately owned land. At that stage, and again in the 1980s with hunger for wood by the world market (notably Japan), the tide turned. The timber industry then pressured the Forest Service and the Bureau of Land Management to start selling logging rights on large parcels of national forests, all of which are public lands.

When they saw the government getting into the timber business in a big way, many Forest Service employees objected but felt helpless to voice their views. They were men who had spent much of their lives in and tending the forests and were more interested in preserving them than "managing" them. This attitude reflected the views of Aldo Leopold, the Forest Service's champion of wilderness protection. He said that it was essential to preserve natural areas for scientific study.

If we know little about the ecology of distant tropical rain forests, we know even less about the Pacific Northwest's forests, which are in our own backyard. The *first* major ecological study of the Pacific Northwest's forests, a slim forty-eight-page report, was prepared in 1981!

The uncontrolled pace of cutting in the old-growth forests has recently caused strong citizen concern and debate with the Forest Service and commercial loggers. Many citizens' groups are saddened, frustrated, and appalled to see the old-growth sequoias, Douglas firs, redwoods, and Sitka spruce tumbling like bowling pins. By law, the Forest Service is not supposed to cut a forest any faster than a secondary forest can replace it. But the Forest Service is cutting 25 percent faster than that.

The Forest Service will soon have to reexamine its goals and practices and ask itself some disturbing questions: To what extent is it possible to carry on massive logging operations *and* protect wilderness areas *and* protect watersheds *and* promote fishing, hunting, hiking, and other recreational activities? As early as 1970, a group of concerned foresters openly criticized the Forest Service for not carrying out its stated policy of multiple-use of public lands.

More recently, a growing number of Forest Service workers have been outspoken in their disapproval of the Forest Service's practices and leadership. One former employee of the Service has said that ". . . we [the U.S. Forest Service] are in the timber industry's hip pocket. We basically support their agenda 99.9 percent of the time."

If there is any doubt about that charge, consider the following: In 1987, pressured by the logging industry, Congress ordered the Forest Service to cut 18 percent more old-growth forests in Washington and Oregon than even the Forest Service itself had planned! In the Siskiyou National Forest, for example, the order is to cut 46.7 percent more than Forest Service plans called for.

In all, the Forest Service carries out logging operations in about 160 forests, selling 70,000 acres of old-growth trees each year. That is enough to fill a line of logging trucks 20,000 miles long. Although it sells the cut timber at a loss in most of its national forests, overall the Service reaps huge profits. In 1987, for example, it took in $267 million. What it loses in most of its forests it makes up for in the highly profitable twelve old-growth forests in Northern California, Oregon, and Washington. Alaska's Tongass National Forest, however, loses money hand over fist. It is the Forest Service's only old-growth money loser, because the Service is stuck with a 50-year contract that requires it to sell highly prized Sitka spruce and Alaska cedar at very low prices to two mills. One, the Alaska Pulp Corporation, is owned by the Japanese. The other, the Ketchikan Pulp Company, is owned by the timber giant Louisiana-Pacific. Louisiana-Pacific's contract requires the Forest Service to sell the ancient trees for about two dollars each. A commercial logger who cuts down an 800-year-old California red cedar gets $10,000 for the tree, and he can cut down a hundred before lunch. According to the Wilderness Society, "the U.S. Forest Service loses an average of 85 cents on the dollar in its clear-cutting in the Tongass National Forest." In some instances it loses 99 cents on the dollar.

In 1989 the Service was given $96 million to bulldoze thousands of miles of new logging roads into public lands. Currently it is campaigning for an additional $2 billion to lay 40,000 miles of new logging roads through virgin forests during the 1990s. The Forest Service has become the world's biggest road-building agency. By 1990 it had carved some 340,000 miles of roads through our national forests, eight times the total mileage of the United States interstate highway network.

The arrogance of both the Forest Service and the timber industry is angering an increasing number of people who want to see at least some of our monarch forests saved. Typical of such arrogance is a statement attributed to Harry Merlo, Chairman of Louisiana-Pacific. "It's ours, it's out there, and we need it all. Now," he reportedly said.

Michael L. Fischer is Executive Director of the Sierra Club, a leading conservation group fighting the timber dealers and the Forest Service. Says Fischer: "Lumber corporations look at trees quite differently from the way you and I do. We know that a forest is *not* a tree farm but a complex, fragile ecosystem, an integral part of the web of life on Earth. But lumber companies can view a lush, verdant forest with spruce, hemlock, or redwoods that have been standing for scores of years, even centuries, and see only board feet of lumber to be 'harvested.' And right now they're on a crash campaign to cut everything in sight." Tree by tree, acre by acre, the ancient and majestic forests of the Pacific Northwest are going.

Chain Saws Versus Feathers

The timber industry's crash campaign to tumble the old-growth forests with all speed has been triggered by a small, two-foot-tall, twenty-two-ounce ball of feathers called the spotted owl. An estimated 3,000 to 5,000 pairs of these shy birds remain in the old-growth forests of the Pacific Northwest. They live among northern California's giant redwood trees and the old-growth spruce and fir of Oregon and Washington. They feed and nest only in the hollows of old-growth trees. In July 1990 the U.S. Fish and Wildlife Service added the spotted owl to its list of threatened or endangered species. This action could mean that millions of acres of public forest lands could be severely restricted or closed to logging.

No hillside is too steep for modern logging technology. If they can't pull a log out by horses or haul it out by truck, they lift it out by helicopter or balloon. The balloon bag contains helium for lift. Upslope, logs are attached to the tether line and ride downslope as a yarder reels in the mainline attached to the tether line. Waiting trucks load the logs at the landing site.

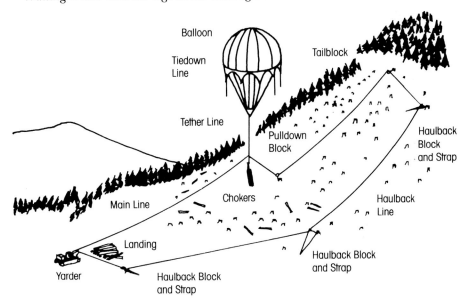

The timber industry's response has been to cut as many old-growth trees as fast as it can, an action it calls "cut and git." From the industry's point of view, closed forests would mean the loss of jobs for cutters, truckers, and mill workers. To calm their fears, President Bush, who calls himself an environmentalist, has favored delays in restricting logging and wants to water down the Endangered Species Act.

While environmental groups express fear that their little spotted owl hero may follow certain other once-endangered species to extinction, loggers applaud the White House move. They vent their fears of restricted cutting by saying that they are the real endangered species, that there are plenty of spotted owls, that their jobs are more important than the spotted owls' survival. Some logging trucks overloaded with old-growth trees sport a sign reading: "Mobile Home for Spotted Owls." Bars in Forks display signs saying that the best use for spotted owls is for toilet paper. Loggers' T-shirts announce, "I love spotted owls . . . FRIED." One logger's truck had a dead spotted owl with an arrow through its head swinging from the rearview mirror. Some loggers say that the spotted owl controversy is nothing more than a way of jacking up the price of lumber.

Such disregard for the wildlife that makes old-growth forests its home enrages environmental groups such as Earth First. An activist group, Earth Firsters drive spikes into old-growth trees, which does not harm the trees but may harm anyone cutting them. They pour sand in the gas tanks of the loggers' trucks, bulldozers, and skidders. They chain themselves to old-growth trees to protect the trees. They form a human chain across a logging road and defy the drivers of logging trucks to run over them.

The Earth Firsters, along with environmental groups that prefer speeches to spikes, deplore the ecological havoc caused by clear-cutting and other reckless logging practices. Catherine Caufield explains why when she describes what has happened to Alaska's Chichagof Island. The Forest Service has permitted loggers to clear-cut old-growth stands over at least seven of the area's vital watersheds. "Gone are dense, low-elevation forests where deer sheltered and fed in winter, and riparian forests where brown bears lived and in whose waters millions of salmon spawned each spring," she reports.

The loggers are supposed to leave ample strips of forest between the clear-cut patches as wildlife refuges for the animals that are displaced. But usually the strips of forest are so narrow that they provide little protection, even when they are not blown down by storms. The 400 square miles of Chichagof Island that have felt the loggers' saws had 200 miles of Forest Service logging roads cut through them in 1990. Spurred on by Congress, the Service plans to build 200 more miles of roads during the next 22 years.

Can Forests Be "Managed"?

The loggers' fears of new regulations and restrictions are understandable. They want their jobs, and they want timber industry jobs for their children. Logging is all they know, and they are not eager to learn other ways to earn a living. Part of their argument is that the need for wood is real and will continue. Where will the wood come from if not from forest management? They point out that clear-cutting is the most economical way to manage forests. We can't wait 200 years for another forest to grow, they argue. Furthermore, what good are the "decadent" old-growth trees? It's better to build a house out of one than just watch it die and rot, they argue. "Bugs, fire, or man are going to harvest the trees. They don't live forever," said one Oregon mill owner. In his vast yard are fifty-five-foot stacks of cut trees, 13,000 trees that once graced 300 acres of mountainside. His mill will gobble up the pile in a mere 6 weeks, at the rate of 320 a day. Log after log is digested by his computer-operated machines that spit out two-by-fours, plywood, planks, particle board, and sawdust faster than you can think. The machines whir 20 hours a day, seven days a week. This scene is repeated in mill town after mill town from Northern California to Alaska. How can anyone expect nature to keep pace?

Forest managers of the Forest Service are trying to speed up growth by using improved genetic varieties of seedlings, fertilizers, and pesticides and by caring for seedlings and young trees. An 80-year-old managed forest, they claim, can produce as much timber as a 500-year-old natural forest. The trees will not be as big, but there will be more of them.

Loggers and mill workers from Northern California to Alaska are troubled, frightened, and confused. The timber industry and environmentalists alike bombard them with statistics they either don't believe or can't understand. Industry says, "Support big timber or you'll lose your job." Environmentalists say, "Support the environment or you'll soon run out of trees to cut and lose your job."

The Forest Service boasts of its plans for "super plantations" that would keep us in timber forever. The plantations would produce fast-growing, genetically improved trees, they say. Critics of the plan call it "voodoo forestry." National Wildlife Federation resource specialist Richard Brown says that all the talk about super plantations is nothing more than a Forest Service "excuse to cut more big old trees now."

No one knows whether tropical rain forest, or a northern or southern coniferous forest, *can* be "managed" for more than a few years. The pine plantations of the eastern United States are now dying after their third cycle of "managed" growth. Europe's famous Black Forest, also a plantation, is dying in its third cycle. The mistake we are making is continuing to clear-cut the monarch forests that remain before finding out whether forest management over the long term is possible.

For more than a century the Pacific Northwest forests seemed inexhaustible. But we have reached that stage in our frenzied rape of the forest when we can grimly imagine the blade of a screaming chain saw chewing its way through the last old-growth Douglas fir in existence.

9
FORESTS
AND PEOPLE —
THE FUTURE

The loggers of the Pacific Northwest call environmentalists "preservationists." The loggers regard these "tree lovers," as they also label environmentalists, as well-off city dwellers who care little for those who log for a living. The "preservationists" view the loggers as pawns of big timber dealers driven by greed as they recklessly destroy what little remains of the nation's natural forest ecosystems. When the two groups clash, there is no communication. They think on different frequencies.

Increasingly the same drama is being played out in what is left of the world's tropical rain forests—by those who cry out for preservation and those who see the rain forests as regions to be conquered and "managed." Is there a middle ground? Is there a "best possible" scenario for the future of the world's remaining forests, everywhere?

Most of this chapter will concentrate on what is happening not in the Amazon Basin or in Africa, where a lot of world attention is presently focused, but in Southeast Asia. The tropical rain forests of this region—Sumatra, Peninsular Malaysia, Borneo, and western Java—are the world's richest, with more diversity than any others. And it is in this region that the most rapid and far-reaching changes in the tropical rain forests are taking place.

"Success" in Peninsular Malaysia?

Malaysia has been remarkable in its ability to coax life out of its generally poor soils. Although the soils are no better than those worked and then abandoned in Amazonia, the Malaysians have managed theirs so well that the region enjoys a high standard of living and has undergone rapid development.

Malaysia's agricultural achievements have involved gradually changing its former rain forest into highly profitable managed forests of crop plants—first coffee, then rubber, and more recently palm oil. In the 1800s the British in Malaysia scouted for profitable local forest products. In 1888 some forests were wisely reserved for sustained timber production in the state of Malacca and on the island of Penang. Hardwood trees were lightly cut for building houses and boats. Earlier, inland tribes had pointed out that certain wild trees, gutta-percha, produced latex, out of which rubber can be made.

By 1877 a lively trade in latex encouraged the British to clear some forest land and plant groves of the rubber tree *Hevea*. The tree was brought over from Brazil. Far removed from their natural insect pests, the trees did well as a single-species plantation plant. So did the native gutta-percha trees. Rubber plantations soon took their place beside already established coffee plantations. By the early 1900s rubber had become an important export crop for Malaysia.

In 1900 Malaysia asked a representative of India's Forest Service, H. C. Hill, to provide advice on the management of Malaysia's tropical rain forests. One thing he noticed was that the virtually seasonless lowland region promoted abundant and continuous growth of seedlings and saplings. Such growth would assure continued replacement of logged trees if the young trees were looked after and if logging proceeded at a reasonable pace. Hill was flabbergasted to count some 4,000 species of trees growing on Peninsular Malaysia. Although the

United States is a hundred times larger than Malaysia, it has barely 400 tree species. Even the seasonal tropical rain forests fail to come close to the diversity of tree species in Malaysia.

Malaysia's well-managed plantations brought wealth and growth to the region. Soon colonization moved increasing numbers of people into the inland forests. Meanwhile, population growth in the major cities of Kuala Lumpur and Ipoh increased the demand for firewood. The demand was easily and conveniently met by cutting into the ample supply of commercially valueless small trees. Those trees had to be cleared anyway in order to assure growth of the favored hardwood trees. By the 1920s, sale of the smaller trees for fuel had become more profitable than sale of the hardwoods. The high species diversity of Malaysia's rain forests gave the forests flexibility. That flexibility, combined with wise management, made it possible to exploit the forest without destroying it.

Out of decades of experience and research, the now classical method of Malaysian rain forest management evolved. Called the Malayan Uniform System, it provides for continued growth of timber-sized trees and for the care of valued seedlings in the understory. Eventually the seedlings grow into a stand of the most commercially favored species. Although the rain forest has been transformed, it has not been destroyed.

In 1957 a new Malaysian government initiated a policy of economic reform, which continues to operate to this day: "Work must be provided for all those who do not own land." Inherent in this policy is the problem of creating enough jobs for the many landless laborers. In order to provide numerous jobs, all but a few sections of the rich lowland tropical rain forest were first cut for valuable timber and then converted to additional rubber and oil palm plantations. Other parcels were earmarked for controlled cutting and the planting of replacement seedlings. Still other parcels were set aside as national parks and nature preserves. The only wild forest that remained untouched was the one growing on the steep slopes of the mountainous interior. Unfortunately, two situations spelled doom in the parcels designated for timber production and regrowth. First, there was reckless use of heavy logging machinery. Second, thousands of poorly supervised, unskilled workers soon began to threaten the health of the valued seedlings, on which natural new growth depended. That situation has continued into the present.

According to Peter S. Ashton of Harvard University, "Those of us who are concerned about the future of tropical forests may decry this most recent change [in Malaysia], which has been disastrous for the old rain-forest resource. But it must also be recognized that the conversion of rain forests to commodity tree crops has allowed Malaysia to become a middle-income nation, bringing unprecedented prosperity to her people and capital for rapid industrialization."

Inspired by Malaysia's success, virtually every Third World nation with a tropical rain forest is determined to cut it down and plant monocultures of coffee, rubber, or palm oil in an attempt to escape the bonds of poverty. These countries might be able to grow their crops, but will they be able to sell them on today's international market? Tropical forest management, even successful management based on the Malayan Uniform System, is one thing; finding a profitable market for coffee, rubber, and palm oil is another. Today the real problem of tree-crop plantations is economic, not agricultural. But that is not to say that agricultural problems do not exist.

After 1981 the price of rubber, palm oil, and many other tropical crops fell sharply. Consequently, the high wages of plantation workers also had to fall if the plantations were to make money. In 1990 Malaysia found itself in just such an economic bind. Its income from plantation crops declined for the first time since the 1940s. Meanwhile, most of Malaysia's forests have been scraped from the land. By 1992 the region will no longer be an exporter of timber, but an importer. Borneo appears to be next in line.

Borneo is the world's third largest island after Greenland and New Guinea. Its northwestern state of Sarawak—roughly one-sixth of the island and slightly smaller than New York state—is one of the largest and richest rain forests in the world. It is the planet's oldest rain forest, estimated at about ten million years old. According to writer Stan Sesser, the Sarawak rain forest has some 20,000 species of flowering plants, several thousand species of trees, hundreds of species of butterflies, and 80 species of mammals, and more than a hundred kinds of fruiting trees. Today the forest is being logged so rapidly and recklessly that it could be gone within five years—and with it the culture of the last of its hunger-gatherers, the shy and gentle Penan. As the trees fall around them, the Penan's rivers become polluted, their homes and food supply destroyed, and their ancestral tribal lands ravaged. Whenever and wherever they try to protect their land they are harassed and imprisoned by a few powerful politicians who daily grow wealthier as they plunder the forest.

Waste and poor management are as rampant in Sarawak as in part of Brazil and eastern Africa. As Sesser writes in a *New Yorker* article, a visitor doesn't have to travel far to see the waste and devastation. During a two-and-a-half-hour boat ride, "for mile after mile logs were piled on either side of the river—tens of thousands of logs, in stacks sometimes twenty feet high. They had been left there to rot. They were logs that had been brought downriver, inspected by the Japanese buyers, and rejected, either because they were the wrong species or because they were marred by defects." Although the government claims it manages the cutting efficiently, the untrained loggers shrug and say they are not told what to cut, so they cut away at anything big and healthy. The bulldozers and skidders then move in and destroy ten trees for every tree logged.

From 1963 through 1985, 30 percent of Sarawak was logged. Today the small state provides almost half the world's export volume of tropical logs.

Southeast Asia's timber boom has just about ended. Randy Hayes, director of the Rainforest Action Network sums it up this way: "At some point, you've got to draw your line in the sand and say, 'Don't cross this line.' Borneo is that line in the sand."

Is There Hope for the Future?

The next fifty years will bring continued and significant loss of tropical rain forests. Those that survive probably will be made national parks or conservation reserves. And for a while, those rooted on steep slopes too rugged to be easily worked or pampered will remain wild. But not for long. The loggers' new technology that employs helicopters and lighter-than-air balloons enables them to reach any mountain slope they target. Forests once regarded as commercially inaccessible are now accessible.

Large portions of the cut regions will be reduced to wasteland like that abandoned by Brazilian ranchers after the toxic weeds take over. And much will be managed plantations on land cleared and then abandoned by settlers who simply give up. As the forests diminish, governments and developers will be pressured to renew spent forest land or to carefully manage the forests that are left. In some instances this pressure will lead to adoption of the Malayan Uniform System of management or some other system whereby logged primary forest is coaxed into even-aged stands of limited species of valued hardwood. Even with the best management, the forests' most valuable asset—their abundant biodiversity and rich gene pools—will be lost.

Meanwhile, pressure on Indian tribes to either join mainstream society or suffer profound cultural degradation probably will increase, with varied effects. Some tribes will die out. Others will cling resolutely to their tribal ways for as long as they can. Still others will try to preserve their customs and at the same time take advantage of modern ways. The Kuna of Panama have chosen the latter route to survival.

After an uprising in 1930 the Kuna were granted recognition of their ancestral land in San Blas. The government strictly forbade anyone but the Kuna to own land there. As a result, the Kuna became the most politically powerful native group in Panama (probably in all of Central America). Many Kuna work outside their territory and have their own trade unions. They have a strong voice in the National Assembly, and they control tourism within their preserve.

The Kuna are not alone in their successful struggle to keep their ancestral land and preserve the substance of their culture. Twenty years ago several Brazilian Indian groups formed the Union of Indian Nations, which fought for the recovery of land illegally taken from them and resisted attempts to degrade their culture. The Union's chief weapon was the ability to communicate its collective plight to the general public through newspapers, radio, and television. These people have found public relations to be more effective than the bow and arrow.

It is unlikely that governments will readily grant to their politically powerless native groups the rights to large tracts of economically valuable land, and organized resistance may in the long run be the best defense the forest people have. Unfortunately, governments tend to overlook or ignore the fact that their forest dwellers are a valuable human resource—for their knowledge of the full range of forest resources and the understanding of their wise use.

According to scientists in Brazil's Amazon research centers, the government should set up buffer zones between Indian reserves and surrounding populated areas to reduce conflict between the Indians and the settlers, miners, and ranchers who often intrude onto Indian land. "If the social problem is not put first," according to one Brazilian official, "we have no solution for the Amazon."

When a hunter of a remote forest tribe hitches a ride on a logging truck, he must feel that part of his culture somehow has slipped away from him.

Guidelines for Action

The years 1987 and 1988 marked the beginning of widespread concern over tropical forest destruction. In the Philippines the government has banned logging in certain areas, cracked down on illegal logging, and raised the royalties timber companies must pay. The Ivory Coast and Ghana have made similar moves. More than 50 nations now have plans to conserve or manage their remaining forests. Guidelines come from the Tropical Forestry Action Plan, sponsored by the World Resources Institute, the United Nations, and the World Bank. A number of private organizations are raising money to buy off Third World nations' debts in exchange for forest conservation and management.

The implementation of plans to preserve certain forest areas and manage others is critical. In addition, international pressure must be applied to stop programs that are wasteful and destructive. For example, the African Development Bank recently agreed to fund a road cut through one of the few remaining rain forest and mangrove habitats of the Ivory Coast. Another planned project will destroy two million acres of primary forest that is home to the Pygmy communities of the Congo. International pressure is needed to force such agencies as the African Development Bank and the World Bank "to stop funding projects that promote senseless forest destruction. Instead they should be supporting sustainable agriculture and forestry efforts that can relieve pressures on primary forests," according to Lester R. Brown of the Worldwatch Institute.

A number of countries—the Philippines and Indonesia among them—now regret their shortsightedness in allowing loggers to destroy vast areas of tropical rain forest in the process of removing as few as two to four trees per acre. Writing in *Scientific American*, Robert Repetto tells us that in spite of regrets over the past and seemingly good intentions for the future on the part of some governments, "not even one-tenth of 1 percent of remaining tropical forests are being actively managed for sustained productivity, according to a recent study commissioned by the International Tropical Timber Organization."

Reforesting the Planet

We must realize that forest destruction and management can no longer be regarded as local affairs that affect only one nation's economy, the jobs of only one region, or the survival of one isolated Indian group. The human population explosion combined with our technological inventiveness and the understandable passion of Third World nations to develop and grow have elevated forest use to a level of global concern. The role of forests in helping regulate the primary greenhouse gas, carbon dioxide, and hence the forests' effect on global climate, are major concerns of the 1990s.

According to the Worldwatch Institute, preservation and expansion of the world's forest cover deserve our urgent attention in order to slow the pace of climate change. The goal: to plant 16 billion trees a year worldwide over the next 15 years. That would forest or reforest 425 million acres. Curbing acid rain and air pollution also will be necessary in order to safeguard forest health. The result could be a decrease of atmospheric carbon dioxide by about one-fourth of current levels as a greater number of trees became available to remove atmospheric carbon dioxide through photosynthesis. "This would slow the pace of warming for several decades, buying precious time to adapt and respond to climate change in other ways," says Brown.

Funding such a massive tree-planting program presents major challenges, Brown adds. It would have to be supported by national leaders, development agencies, corporations, nongovernment organizations, community groups, and individual citizens. Kenya's Greenbelt Movement has mobilized farmers and schoolchildren to plant more than two million trees. Applied Energy Services of the United States is helping to pay for a reforestation project in Guatemala to compensate for a power plant it is building in Connecticut. With help from the U.S. Agency for International Development, more than thirty-five million seedlings were planted in Haiti between 1982 and 1987. The American Forestry Association intends to plant some 100 million trees in cities and suburbs around the United States between now and 1992.

Protection Versus Management

Little more than a century has passed since man began tinkering with forests in an attempt to manage them, to mold them to his purpose. When viewed as an ecological system, the forests remain little known to us, yet we presume to be able to "manage" them; that is, to use them for our narrow economic designs. We do not know for certain that we can manage a forest, except over a relatively short time. As soon as we try, we make the forest unstable and dependent on our care. A natural forest needs no such care and is self-sustaining. As mentioned earlier, the managed pine plantations of the eastern United States are dying after only their third cycle of growth. In German and Scandinavian plantations the trees are dying. The Forest Service also reports a marked rise in tree deaths on tree plantations in the southeastern United States. Some contend that the deaths are due to acid rain. Others say that intensive "management" over several centuries is the cause. Although we can grow *trees,* we have not yet learned to grow a *forest.* Weather, climate, air quality, adequate biodiversity with its numerous and essential plant-animal associations, and many other conditions that we may not even be aware of are beyond our control, beyond our present ability to manage.

Foresters, and even some of the timber dealers themselves, are beginning to think that maybe the best way to "manage" a forest is to copy the ways of the natural forest. Rather than concentrate on only one or two species, make the forest diverse. Don't rake it clean, but leave fallen limbs, dead trees, and other organic remains in place. Cover over the old logging roads. Then when the trees are ripe, don't clearcut. Instead cut patches of the forest here and there, mimicking what nature does when fires are started by lightning. Then get out and stay out for twenty years, fifty years, a hundred years, for however long it takes the forest to renew itself, by itself. Meanwhile, leave vast tracks of forest forever undisturbed. These will be the laboratories from which we learn what a forest is and what it does in its own way in its own time. In the long run, that may be the most economical use of a forest, and the only way a forest can be "managed."

Such undisturbed forests are climax vegetation zones that cannot be "improved." They sustain themselves with the optimum diversity of plants and animals living in association. There is nothing to "manage" in such a system. A tropical rain forest is the most diverse and, because of its diversity, the most splendid natural living system on earth. There is no possible way to improve it. At best we can protect a fair share of the world's remaining primary forests simply by leaving them alone. If they are to change, let them change in their own way in their own time. We cannot hurry a forest; we must learn to adjust our wants and needs to its pace.

To live in harmony with nature, civilized human beings will have to learn to control their human population so that our numbers do not overwhelm nature. Forest people learned that lesson thousands of years ago and have regulated their numbers accordingly. They know they cannot take from the environment more than the environment has to offer.

Postscript

FORDLANDIA: A FOREIGNER'S DREAM

Attempts to "manage" a tropical rain forest have an interesting history. And we are little closer to the answer today than a half century ago when automobile king Henry Ford's dream to tame a Brazilian rain forest turned into a nightmare. While such management schemes have brought misfortune to the would-be managers, they have been a source of amused bewilderment for those who know something about tropical rain forests and their people.

It is as if Ford had heard the dream of then President Theodore Roosevelt. On traveling through the Amazon, Roosevelt was astounded by what he saw: "Surely such a rich and fertile land cannot be permitted to remain idle, to lie as a tenantless wilderness," he wrote. Ford decided to become a tenant and reap riches. He had visions of operating a huge rubber plantation that would supply rubber for the tires needed by the many automobiles he was selling.

In 1926, with the blessing of the Brazilian government, Ford formed the Ford Industrial Company of Brazil. He would build an enormous rubber plantation that would employ many Brazilian workers in exchange for free use of 2,471,000 acres of land. Under the arrangement, Ford's company would not have to pay taxes for 50 years, and after 12 years the company would begin to share profits with Brazil.

Fordlandia was the new community's name. It had a beautiful waterfront harbor, a well-equipped hospital, a school, cozy houses for some 4,000 workers, a nursery for tree seedlings, a sawmill, and five miles of railroad. The sawmill cut fine tropical hardwoods, which were shipped to the United States. Nearly half a million rubber trees were planted on some 7,000 acres of cleared land. By 1936 the first trees were ready for tapping.

But all had not gone well. The land around Fordlandia was hilly, and as the slopes were deforested erosion gullied the soil and flooded low-lying areas of the community. The fine hardwood trees soon were all cut, and the sawmill had to be closed. South American leaf blight invaded Ford's neatly rowed plantation trees and killed most of the young ones. He decided to start a new plantation elsewhere.

The new site, ten times larger than the first one, was named Belterra. The site was well situated and the soil well drained. This time Ford planted three million trees, two million of which were Malaysian seedlings grafted onto native roots, a tedious and expensive procedure. The grafting was designed to make the seedlings disease-resistant. The ambitious new operation was so big that Ford could not find enough workers. First, he lacked the technical knowledge to run a plantation. Then, too late, he found that he lacked sufficient knowledge about his Brazilian workers. He made the mistake of treating them the way he treated his midwestern workers back home. Instead of providing them with their customary native food, he imported food from Detroit. He also introduced square dancing, which the workers didn't understand or want. And he insisted that they work tightly scheduled hours. He could not understand that Amazonian natives were not accustomed to the kind of regimented life led by his auto workers in the United States. By 1941, 2,723 rubber tappers worked the plantation, but 11,000 were needed to reach production goals.

A labor shortage, continued bouts with leaf blight, the high cost of grafting, and other woes forced the operation to close. Over the years, Ford had put more than nine million dollars into Fordlandia and Belterra. In 1945 Henry Ford II sold the entire mess to the Brazilian government for a half million dollars. Over the nineteen-year-period Ford had failed to produce enough rubber to make a pencil eraser.

Explanation 1
HOW POPULATION MOMENTUM WORKS

Here is a graphic example (from Paul Ehrlich) of how population momentum works:

Suppose that India miraculously managed to achieve in its population growth what is called "replacement reproduction" around the year 2025. Replacement reproduction means that each couple has no more than two children—only enough children to replace the mother and father. Because India has so many young people, even if the young couples have only two children each, the population will continue to grow for about 60 years. At the end of that time, late in the next century, there will be fewer young people and more old people. At that time the number of births will begin to equal the number of deaths each year. Not until then will India's population begin to stabilize. But by then it will have zoomed from 853 million in 1990 to two billion! That was the population of the entire world in the year 1930! How is India to feed that massive number of mouths? Imagine the catastrophic starvation that two or three years of drought would bring. Also consider the Indian subcontinent having to support 300 million Pakistanis and

300 million Bangladeshis. That will be 10 times as many people as now live in the United States. The probable results of such a jamming together of so many people are war, massive deaths by starvation, and unimaginable poverty.

Consider our own situation in the United States. Some argue that with our current birth rate the U.S. population will soon start to decline. Not quite. Even if American women had children below replacement level, it would still be fifty years before we reached a stable population. And during that time our population would keep growing—in the year 2033 there would be 67 million more people than our present 250 million. Those who tend to play down the seriousness of world population growth by focusing on only a few rich nations (Germany and Denmark) that have reached replacement reproduction simply do not know what they are talking about.

In 1985, the governments of China, India, Bangladesh, Egypt, Kenya, and other nations signed a Statement on Population Stabilization, part of which reads: *"If unprecedented population growth continues, future generations of children will not have adequate food, housing, medical care, education, earth resources, and employment opportunities."* The United States was conspicuously absent at the signing. President Reagan felt that it was impolitic to go around telling people to have fewer children. Such action does not win votes.

Explanation 2
HOW PHOTOSYNTHESIS WORKS

During the day green plants—grasses, shrubs, and trees—carry on a remarkable chemical transformation called photosynthesis. Tiny green structures (chloroplasts) inside the leaves combine carbon dioxide from the air with water from the soil and drive the chemical reaction with the energy of sunlight. In the process, the leaves give off free oxygen to the air as a by-product. The reaction also produces glucose, a sugar that is used to nourish the plant. Glucose also provides nourishment for animals that eat the green plants:

$$CO_2 \quad + \quad H_2O \quad ----> \quad [CH_2O] \quad + \quad H_2O \quad + \quad O_2$$

Carbon dioxide	Water vapor		Glucose	Water		Oxygen

The green leaves of all plants make sugar during the daylight hours. The sugar flows down the stem and into the roots. In that way, cells throughout the plant are nourished. When light levels are too low or absent, as at night, the photosynthetic machinery of a green plant is shut down.

Glossary

Adaptation The condition of a plant or animal population being in tune with its environment, or its ability to adjust to changes in the environment (scarcity of food, or change in climate, for example). Sometimes the environmental changes are so severe that no individuals of the population can survive, and the population dies out. In other cases, when the change is less severe, certain individuals that are "fitter" than the others are able to survive and pass on their fitness to their offspring. In that way, the population as a group becomes adapted to the new environment.

Algae Any of many green plants capable of photosynthesis and belonging to the group known as thallophytes. They include seaweeds and various freshwater plants such as green pond scum.

Agroforestry The practice of growing trees in association with various food crops and animals in order to maximize productive use of the land where both forest products and food are important to the economy. Agroforestry played an important economic role among certain groups of the Mayan cultures a thousand or more years ago, and it could be practiced today to great advantage in many Third World tropical forest cultures.

Anthropology The "study of man," including social organization, relationship to the environment, customs and beliefs, language, and physical aspects of people living today and people who lived long ago.

Archaeology The study of the history and cultures of peoples who lived in the past, which involves discovering and interpreting the material remains they left behind.

Bacteria   A wide range of primitive and very ancient organisms that are neither plant nor animal. They depend for nutrition on other organisms and their by-products. They drift about in the air ready to infect us with disease; they live in the soil and make it fertile; they live in the ooze of the lake bottom without oxygen; and they live on and in our bodies where they help digest our food and rid us of waste matter.

Biodiversity   A measure of the richness of species of plants and animals, their diversity and variety, in a given ecosystem. (See also **Diversity**)

Biomapping   The cataloging of all plant and animal species living in a given ecosystem.

Botanist   A scientist who specializes in the study of plants.

Canopy   The uppermost layer of a forest where the trees receive the most intense sunlight and are exposed to the extremes of weather.

Cell   The smallest organized unit of living matter recognized by biologists. All living organisms are composed of cells. Some organisms, such as a paramecium and an amoeba, are a single cell.

Climate   A region's weather averaged over a long span of time. From the Greek word *klima*, meaning "slope" or "incline," and referring to the degree of slant of the Sun's rays relative to Earth's surface.

Climax Forest   An ecological community in which diversity of plant and animal species has peaked and stabilized. The species of a climax community tend to be less flexible and less adaptable to environmental changes than are species of earlier communities, partly because most ecological niches have been filled. There is little room for newcomers until environmental change opens new niches.

Coniferous Forest   A forest composed mainly of cone-bearing trees that do not shed their needle-leaves, such as pine, fir, and spruce trees.

Consumer   Any organism that relies on "producer" organisms for food. Consumers eat plants, or they eat other consumers. Plants are producers because they manufacture food through photosynthesis. They store that food, which is then available to those who feed on the producer.

Culture   The customs, equipment, techniques, manufactures, ideas, language, and beliefs of a people.

Deciduous Plants   Groups of trees and shrubs that respond to environmental change by shedding their leaves seasonally.

Decomposers   Organisms that function as agents of decay—mostly bacteria and fungi, which feed on the dead remains of plants and animals alike.

Delta   A deposit of soil, sand, clay, and other alluvial material carried by river water and deposited at the mouth of the river. Deltas usually are triangular in shape and are named after *delta*, the fourth letter of the Greek alphabet, which is a triangle.

Diversity   The many different kinds of animal and plant species that have evolved over the past 3 billion or so years. Scientists have classified more than 1,200,000 different animal species and at least 500,000 species of plants. Each year thousands of newly discovered species are added to the lists.

Ecology   The science of relationships between living organisms and their environment.

Ecosystem   A community of organisms plus all aspects of their physical and chemical environment.

Element   A substance made up entirely of the same kinds of atoms. Such a substance cannot be broken down into a simpler substance by chemical means. Examples are gold, oxygen, carbon, and chlorine.

Environment   The total of physical, chemical, and biological factors that may influence an organism.

Epiphyte   A plant that attaches to and uses another plant for support but does not obtain nourishment parasitically from the other plant. Examples include lichens, mosses, and orchids.

Erosion   The long-term effects of heat, water, wind, ice, and rain that wear away or chemically dissolve solid rock. The eroded particles are called sediments. Sediments may be formed by mechanical action or by chemical or biochemical processes. Erosion also occurs when rains wash soil into streams and rivers, or when unconsolidated soil is transported by wind.

Evolution   The various patterns of biological change that ultimately cause the success (adaptation) or failure (extinction) of species and produce new species of plants and animals. Biological evolution continues to take place today. Charles Darwin and Alfred Russell Wallace are credited with developing the basic principles of organic evolution.

Extinction   The total disappearance of an entire species or major group of organisms, such as trilobites or dinosaurs. Once a species has become extinct, it is gone forever.

Fossils   The remains of once-living organisms. Fossils may be bits of bone or teeth or even footprints or other imprints left from long ago. Most fossils are found in sedimentary rock and usually are more than 10,000 years old.

Fungi   Simple organisms that lack chlorophyll; many are microscopic. The fungi include mushrooms, molds, rusts, and yeasts.

Gene   The biological unit of inheritance that determines a particular trait, such as hair color, tallness, or general physical appearance of an individual. Genes are clustered as chromosomes and are composed of DNA.

Gene Pool   Collectively, all of the various genes present in the individuals of a population and available for combination as the individuals mate and reproduce.

Genus   A broad grouping of organisms, all of which have certain characteristics in common but which belong to different species. For example, there are various species of the genus *Homo*. *Homo sapiens* means "wise man" and refers to modern humans. According to the principles of evolution, all members of the same genus are descended from a common ancestor.

Geologic Time   The time that has passed since Earth's history began. It involves millions and billions of years, very much longer than our imagination can grasp.

Glacier   Any mass of moving land ice formed out of compacted snow.

Glucose   A sugar used as food by plants and animals alike. Glucose is produced by green plants when they combine carbon dioxide and water vapor in the presence of light as an energy source. In the process called photosynthesis, the green plant gives off oxygen as a by-product.

Greenhouse Effect   Global warming that results from greenhouse gases. The principal greenhouse gas is carbon dioxide. The gases trap long-wave (heat) radiation emitted from Earth's surface and thereby prevent radiation of the heat into space.

Greenhouse Gases   Those gases that hang in Earth's atmosphere and trap heat radiated from Earth's surface. They are largely the result of human activity. They include carbon dioxide, produced by the burning of fossil fuels and cleared forests, which accounts for about half the man-made greenhouse gases; water vapor, a dry gas produced when water evaporates; methane, produced by bacteria breaking down dead matter, which contributes 15 to 20 percent of the man-made greenhouse gases; chlorofluorocarbons (CFSs), used, for example, in refrigeration, air conditioning, and insulation, which contribute another 20 percent of the man-made greenhouse gases; and nitrous oxide, produced by microbes in the soil, chemical fertilizers, slash-and-burn farming, and fossil-fuel emissions, which contributes about 5 percent of the man-made emissions. Carbon dioxide hangs in the air as long as 100 years before breaking down; methane, 10 years; CFCs as long as 400 years; nitrous oxide, 180 years.

Habitat   The physical environment in which a species lives, together with all the plant and animal organisms to be found there.

Humus   The top layer of soil resulting from the decay of plant and animal remains. Humus-rich soil is the best for rapid and healthful plant growth.

Ice Age   Any extended period of time during which a substantial portion of Earth's surface is covered by "permanent" ice. At least seven major ice ages have occurred during the past 700,000 years; the last ice age reached its peak about 18,000 years ago.

Liana   A tropical forest climbing plant that has a long, woody, ropelike stem.

Mammal   Any vertebrate animal that has warm blood and a covering of hair, gives birth to its young (with two exceptions), and suckles its young.

Monoculture   The practice of growing principally, or exclusively, one crop, instead of using the land to grow a mixture of different kinds of plants.

Mutualism   A biological association in which two different species live together to the mutual benefit of each other.

Natural Selection   A process whereby the environment favors for survival those individuals that are the fittest, or best adapted to environmental conditions. While the less fit tend to be selected against and do not survive, those that are more fit live to reproduce offspring and so pass their fitness on to the next generation.

Paleo-Indians   Groups of people who entered the Americas from Asia until 5,000 B.C. Most researchers think that the Paleo-Indians crossed to the New World over a sprawling land bridge that existed near the end of the last glacial period. Recent evidence suggests that Paleo-Indians may have been in South America at least 30,000 years ago, and possibly earlier.

Photosynthesis   The process by which green plants build molecules of sugar out of water vapor and carbon dioxide from the atmosphere in the presence of sunlight and the green pigment chlorophyll. In the process oxygen is given off as a by-product. Green plants supply most of the world's living organisms with food.

Population Momentum   The continued rapid growth of a population after the population's death rate equals its birth rate, due to the relatively large number of young people of reproductive age. Population momentum lessens as the ratio of younger people to older people decreases.

Primary Forest   Virgin, untouched forest, such as the centuries-old forests of Sitka spruce, Douglas fir, and California redwoods.

Producers   Organisms that carry out photosynthesis and in the process produce glucose. The producers and the organisms that eat them use the glucose as food.

Reptiles   Cold-blooded vertebrates, such as lizards, snakes, and alligators. The Cretaceous period marked the peak of the reptiles' success; it was dominated by the dinosaurs.

Respiration   The process in which oxygen is used to drive chemical (metabolic) reactions that in turn produce carbon dioxide as a waste product.

Secondary Forest   A forest that grows and replaces a destroyed primary forest; secondary forests are fast-growing and lack the biodiversity of a primary forest. The soil of a secondary forest usually is poor due to the erosion that took place when the primary forest was destroyed.

Sediments   The loose bits and pieces of clay, mud, sand, gravel, lime, and other earth materials. Some pile up century after century and become squeezed by the great weight of new sediments above. Eventually, heaps of such sediments may be thrust up as new mountains.

Species   Any one kind of animal or plant group, each member of which is like every other member in certain important ways. All populations of such a group are capable of interbreeding and producing healthy offspring that are, in turn, capable of reproducing.

Transpiration   The loss of water from the internal tissues of plants through openings, mostly in the leaves.

Variation   Those biological differences among the individuals of a population. These variations lead to evolutionary change.

Weathering   The erosion of rocks and soil by frost and other weather conditions. Small pieces of rock on mountains are continually being eroded and carried away by the wind and streams as sediment particles, many of which are carried far out onto the ocean floors. Mechanical weathering is the physical breakdown of rock, by frost, for example. Chemical weathering is the chemical breakdown of rock by acid rain that is produced naturally or by the pollutants released by factories. Acid rain damages vast stretches of forest and erodes statues of stone and the stone facings of buildings.

Understory   The level of foliage in a forest that extends downward from the canopy.

Water Vapor   The gaseous form of water, a dry gas.

Further Reading

BOOKS

Aiken, S. R., C. H. Leigh, T. R. Leibach, and M. R. Moss. *Development and Environment in Peninsular Malaysia*. Singapore: McGraw-Hill, 1982.

Blaikie, P., and H. Brookfield. *Land Degradation and Society*. New York: Methuen, 1987.

Bolin, B., E. T. Degens, S. Kempe, and P. Ketner, eds. *The Global Carbon Cycle*. New York: John Wiley & Sons, 1979.

Brown, Lester R. *State of the World*. New York: W. W. Norton & Co., Inc., 1990.

Burley, F. W., and P. Hazlewood. *Tropical Forest Action Plan, Journal 86*, the Annual Report of the World Resources Institute. Washington, D.C.: The World Resources Institute, 1987.

Caufield, C. *In the Rainforest*. New York: Knopf, 1986.

Cavalli-Sforza, L. L., ed. *African Pygmies*. New York: Academic Press, 1986.

Denslow, Julie Sloan, and Christine Padoch, eds. *People of the Tropical Rain Forest*. Berkeley: University of California Press in association with Smithsonian Institution Traveling Exhibition Service, 1989.

Duffy, K. *Children of the Forest*. New York: Dodd, Mead and Company, 1984.

Durrell, L. *State of the Ark: An Atlas of Conservation in Action*. Garden City, N.Y.: Doubleday, 1986.

Ehrlich, Paul R., and Anne H. Ehrlich. *The Population Explosion*. New York: Simon and Schuster, 1990.

Flenley, John R. *The Equatorial Rain Forest: A Geological History.* Boston: Butterworths, 1979.

Forsyth, A., and K. Miyata. *Tropical Nature.* New York: Scribner's, 1984.

Gallant, Roy A. *Earth's Changing Climate.* New York: Four Winds Press, 1979.

———. *Before the Sun Dies: The Story of Evolution.* New York: Macmillan, 1989.

———. *The Peopling of Planet Earth: Human Population Growth Through the Ages.* New York: Macmillan, 1990.

———. *Our Restless Earth.* New York: Franklin Watts, 1986.

Goulet, D. *The Cruel Choice: A New Concept in the Theory of Development.* New York: Atheneum, 1978.

Hames, R. B., and W. T. Vickers, eds. *Adaptive Responses of Native Amazonians.* New York: Academic Press, 1983.

Hemming, J., ed. *The Frontier After a Decade of Colonization.* Vol. 2. *Change in the Amazon Basin.* Manchester: Manchester University Press, 1985.

Hoage, R. J., ed. *Animal Extinctions: What Everyone Should Know.* Washington, D.C.: Smithsonian Institute Press, 1985.

Jordan, C. F. *Nutrient Cycling in Tropical Forest Ecosystems.* New York: John Wiley and Sons, 1985.

Kormondy, Edward J. *Concepts of Ecology.* 3rd ed. Englewood Cliffs, N.J.: Prentice-Hall, Inc., 1984.

———. ed. *International Handbook of Pollution Control.* New York: Greenwood Press, 1989.

Lamb, F. B. *Wizard of the Upper Amazon: The Story of Manuyel Cordova-Rios.* Berkeley: North Atlantic Books, 1971.

Longman, K. A., and J. Jenik. *Tropical Forest and its Environment.* 2nd ed. New York: Longman Scientific and Technical, 1987.

Mabberly, D. J. *Tropical Rain Forest Ecology.* London: Blackie, 1983.

McCormick, Jack. *The Life of the Forest.* New York: McGraw-Hill Book Company, 1966.

Meggers, B. J. *Amazonia: Man and Culture in a Counterfeit Paradise.* Chicago: Aldine Publishing Company, 1971.

Moran, E. F. *Developing the Amazon*. Bloomington, Ind.: Indiana University Press, 1981.

Myers, Norman. *The Primary Source: Tropical Forests and Our Future*. New York: W. W. Norton & Co., Inc., 1984.

———. *The Sinking Ark*. New York: Pergamon Press, 1979.

Perera, V., and R. D. Bruce. *The Last Lords of Palenque: The Lacandon Mayas of the Mexican Rain Forest*. Boston: Little, Brown & Co., 1982.

Perry, D. *Life Above the Jungle Floor*. New York: Simon and Schuster, 1986.

Prance, G. T., and T. E. Lovejoy, eds. *Amazonia*. Oxford: Pergamon Press, 1985.

Repetto, R., and M. Gillis, eds. *Public Policies and the Misuse of Forest Resources*. Cambridge: Cambridge University Press, 1990.

Schneider, Stephen H. *Global Warming: Are We Entering the Greenhouse Century?* San Francisco: Sierra Club Books, 1989.

———, and R. Londer. *The Coevolution of Climate and Life*. San Francisco: Sierra Club Books, 1984.

Shultes, Richard, and R. F. Raffauf. *The Healing Forest*. Dioscorides Press, 1990.

Shane, D. R. *Hoofprints on the Forest: Cattle Ranching and the Destruction of Latin America's Tropical Forests*. Philadelphia: Institute for the Study of Human Issues, 1986.

The Vanishing Forest: The Human Consequences of Deforestation. A Report for the Independent Commission on International Humanitarian Issues. London and New Jersey: Zed Books Ltd.

Wilmsen, Edwin N. *A Political Economy of the Kalahari*. Chicago: University of Chicago Press, 1990.

Wilson, E. O., ed. *Biodiversity*. Washington, D.C.: National Academy Press, 1988.

Woodward, F. I. *Climate and Plant Distribution*. Cambridge: Cambridge University Press, 1987.

World Resources—1990–91: A Guide to the Global Environment. New York: Oxford University Press, 1990.

ARTICLES

Abelson, Philip H. "Uncertainties About Global Warming." *Science*, 30 March 1990, p. 1529.

Alper, Joe. "Environmentalists: Ban the (Population) Bomb." *Science*, 31 May 1991, p. 1247.

Bailey, Robert C. "The Efe: Archers of the Rain Forest." *National Geographic*, November 1989, pp. 664–686.

Baker, Lawrence A., et al. "Acidic Lakes and Streams in the United States: The Role of Acidic Deposition." *Science*, 24 May 1991, pp. 1151–1153.

Booth, Robert. "Dominica, Difficult Paradise." *National Geographic*, June 1990, pp. 100–120.

Caufield, Catherine. "The Rain Forests." *The New Yorker*, 14 January 1985, pp. 41–101.

———. "The Ancient Forest." *The New Yorker*, 14 May 1990, pp. 46–84.

Crutzen, Paul J., and Meinrat O. Andreae. "Biomass Burning in the Tropics: Impact on Atmospheric Chemistry and Biogeochemical Cycles." *Science*, 21 December 1990, pp. 1669–1678.

Detweiler, R. P., and C. A. S. Hall. "Tropical Forests and the Global Carbon Cycle." *Science* Vol. 239: pp. 42–47.

Devillers, Carole. "What Future for the Wayanas?" *National Geographic*, January 1983, pp. 66–83.

Ellis, William S. "Rondônia: Brazil's Imperiled Rain Forest." *National Geographic*, December 1988, pp. 772–799.

———. "Africa's Stricken Sahel." *National Geographic*, August 1987, pp. 140–179.

Ewel, J., et al. "Slash and Burn Impacts on a Costa Rican West Forest Site." *Ecology* 62:1981, pp. 816–829.

Findley, Rowe. "Endangered Old-Growth Forests." *National Geographic*, September 1990, pp. 106–136.

Flavin, Christopher. "Slowing Global Warming: A Worldwide Strategy." Worldwatch Paper 91. Worldwatch Institute, October 1989.

French, Hilary F. "Clearing the Air: A Global Agenda." Worldwatch

94. Washington, D.C.: Worldwatch Institute, January 1990.

Gibbons, Boyd. "Missouri's Garden of Consequence." *National Geographic*, August 1990, pp. 124–140.

Gup, Ted. "Owl vs. Man." *Time*, 25 June 1990, pp. 55–63.

Halle, Francis. "A Raft Atop the Rain Forest." *National Geographic*, October 1990, pp. 129–138.

Headland, Thomas N. "Paradise Revised." *The Sciences*, September/October 1990, pp. 45–50.

Houghton, R. A., and G. M. Woodwell. "Global Climate Change." *Scientific American*, April 1989, pp. 36–44.

"How Climate Changes." *The Economist*, April 7, 1990, p. 13.

Hughes, Carol and David. "Teeming Life of a Rain Forest." *National Geographic*, January 1983, pp. 49–65.

Hutterer, K. L. "The Natural and Cultural History of Southeast Asian Agriculture." *Anthropos*, 1979, pp. 169–212.

Janowski, Pat. "Mapping the Immeasurable." *Scientific American*, July 1990, pp. 24–25.

Linden, E. "Playing with Fire." *Time*, September 18, 1989, pp. 76–85.

Matthews, Samuel W. "Under the Sun: Is Our World Warming?" *National Geographic*, October 1990, pp. 66–99.

McIntyre, Loren. "Urueu-Wau-Wau Indians: Last Days of Eden." *National Geographic*, December 1988, pp. 800–817.

Mohnen, V. A. "The Challenge of Acid Rain." *Scientific American* 259(2): pp. 30–38.

Monastersky, Richard. "The Fall of the Forest." *Science News* 138: pp. 40–41.

Nectoux, Francois, and Yoichi Kuroda. "Timber from the South Seas: An Analysis of Japan's Tropical Environmental Impact." Gland, Switzerland, World Wildlife Fund International, 1989.

Nelson-Horchler, Joani. "Please Save the Rain Forests." *Industry Week*, 18 June 1990, p. 85.

O'Connor, Raymond J. "Fading Melody." *The Sciences*, January/February 1991, pp. 36–41.

Postel, Sandra, and Lori Heise. "Reforesting the Earth." Worldwatch

Paper 83. Washington, D.C.: Worldwatch Institute, April 1988.

Reiss, Spencer. "The Last Days of Eden." *Newsweek*, December 3, 1990, pp. 48–50.

Repetto, Robert. "Deforestation in the Tropics." *Scientific American*, April 1990, pp. 36–42.

———. "The Forest for the Trees? Government Policies and the Misuse of Forest Resources." World Resources Institute, 1988.

Revelle, R. "Carbon Dioxide and World Climate." *Scientific American* 247(2): pp. 35–43.

Richards, P. W. "The Tropical Rain Forest." *Scientific American*, December 1973, pp. 58–67.

Roberts, Leslie. "Ranking the Rain Forests." *Science,* 29 March 1991, pp. 1559–1560.

Romme, W. H. and D. G. Despain. "The Yellowstone Fires." *Scientific American*, November 1989, pp. 37–46.

Royte, Elizabeth. "The Ant Man." *New York Times Magazine*, July 22, 1990, p. 17.

Schlesinger, W. H., ed. "Forest Decline." A special feature in *Ecology* 259(2): pp. 30–38.

Schneider, S. H. "The Greenhouse Effect: Science and Policy." *Science* 243: pp. 771–781.

Schulze, E. D. "Air Pollution and Forest Decline in a Spruce (*Picea abies*) Forest." *Science* 244: pp. 776–783.

Seattle Times and Seattle Post-Intelligencer's Sunday, August 19, 1990 edition published comprehensive coverage of clear-cutting in the state of Washington.

Sesser, Stan. "The Bornec Rain Forest." *The New Yorker*, 27 May 1991, pp. 42–67.

Smith, Nigel. "Wood: An Ancient Fuel with a New Future." Worldwatch Paper 42. Washington, D.C.: Worldwatch Institute, January 1981.

Springen, Karen. "Old Allies in a Timber War." *Newsweek* 24: September 1990, p. 31.